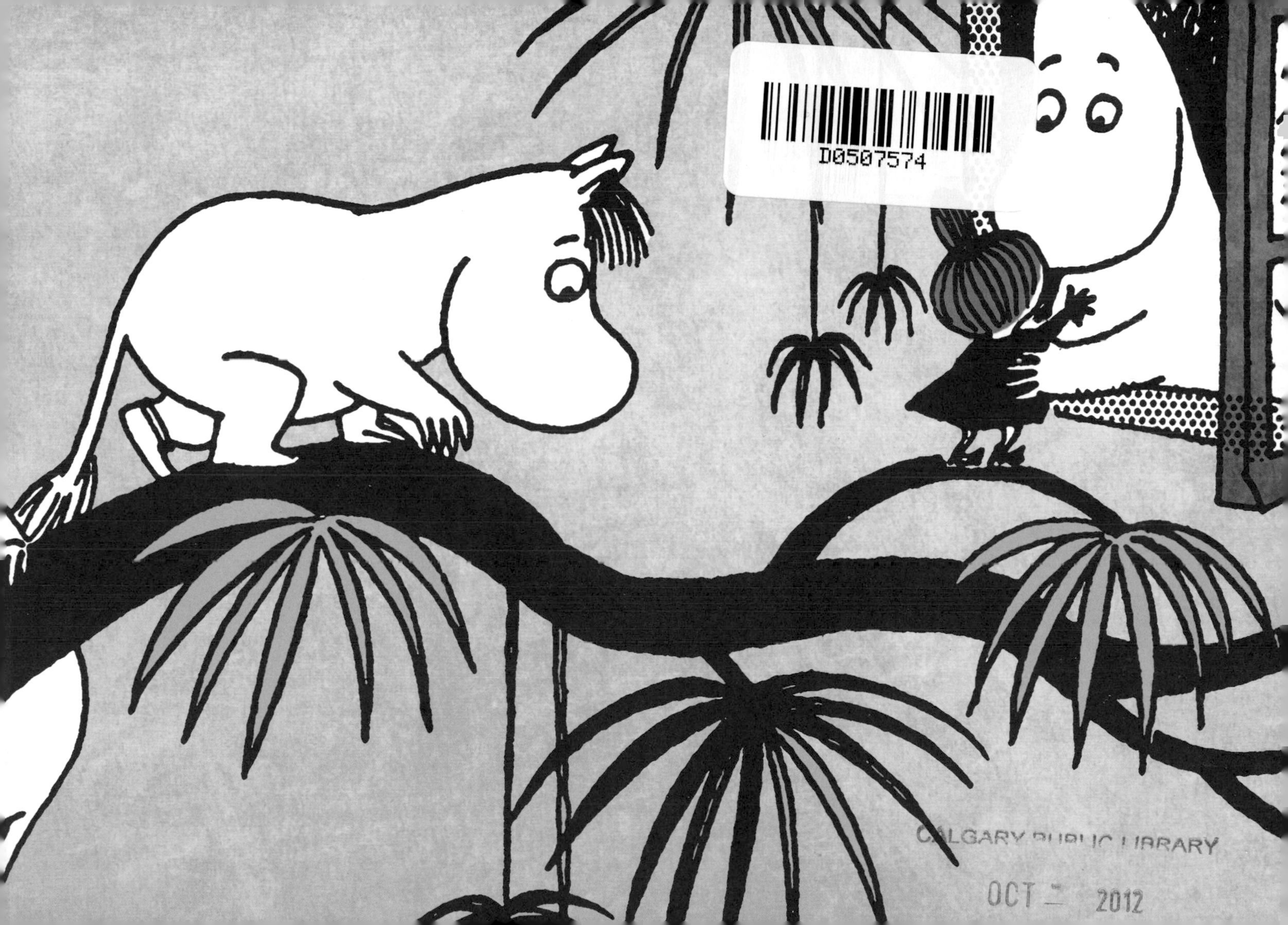

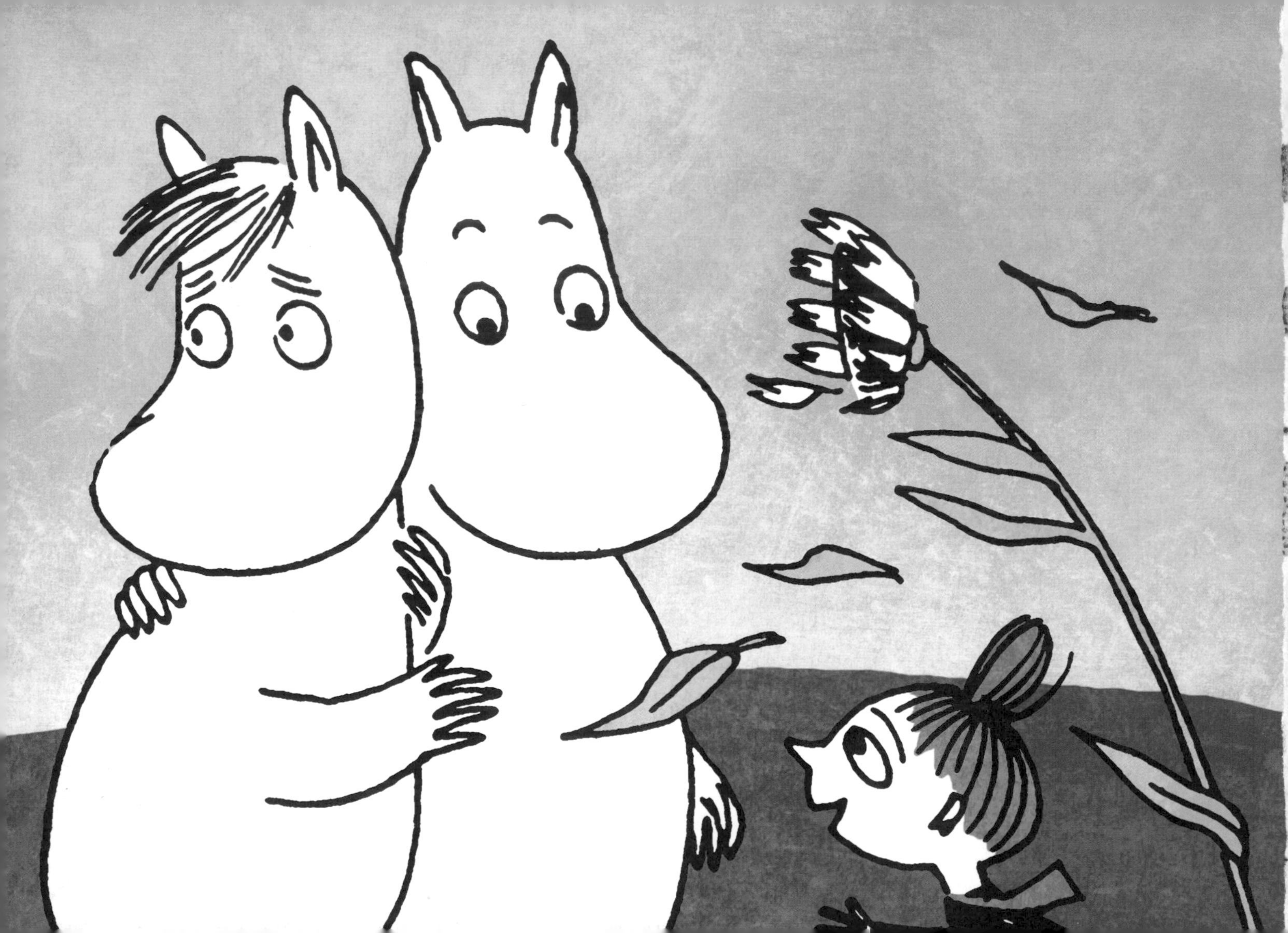

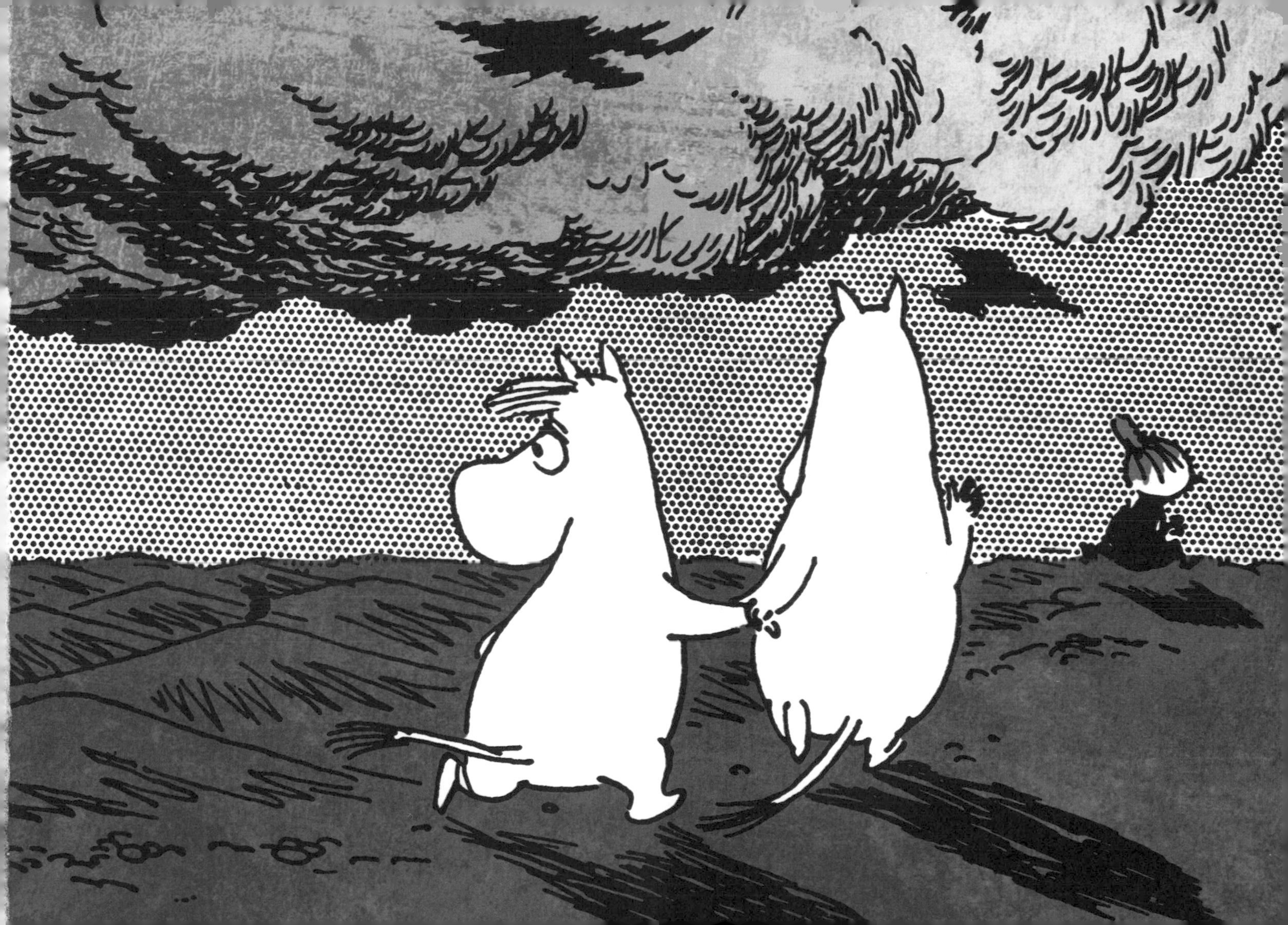

Enfant is an imprint of Drawn & Quarterly.

Enfant
Post Office Box 48056
Montreal, Quebec
Canada H2V 4S8
www.drawnandquarterly.com

First edition: August 2012
Printed in Malaysia
10 9 8 7 6 5 4 3 2 1

Library and Archives Canada Cataloguing in Publication
Jansson, Tove
Moominvalley Turns Jungle / Tove Jansson.
ISBN 978-1-77046-097-3
1. Graphic novels. I. Title.
PZ7.7.J35M65 2012 j741.5'94897
C2012-902521-6

Distributed in the USA by:
Farrar, Straus and Giroux
18 West 18th Street
New York, NY 10011
Orders: 888.330.8477

Distributed in Canada by:
Raincoast Books
2440 Viking Way
Richmond, BC V6V 1N2
Orders: 800.663.5714

Distributed in the United Kingdom by:
Publishers Group UK
63-66 Hatton Garden
London
EC1N 8LE
info@pguk.co.uk

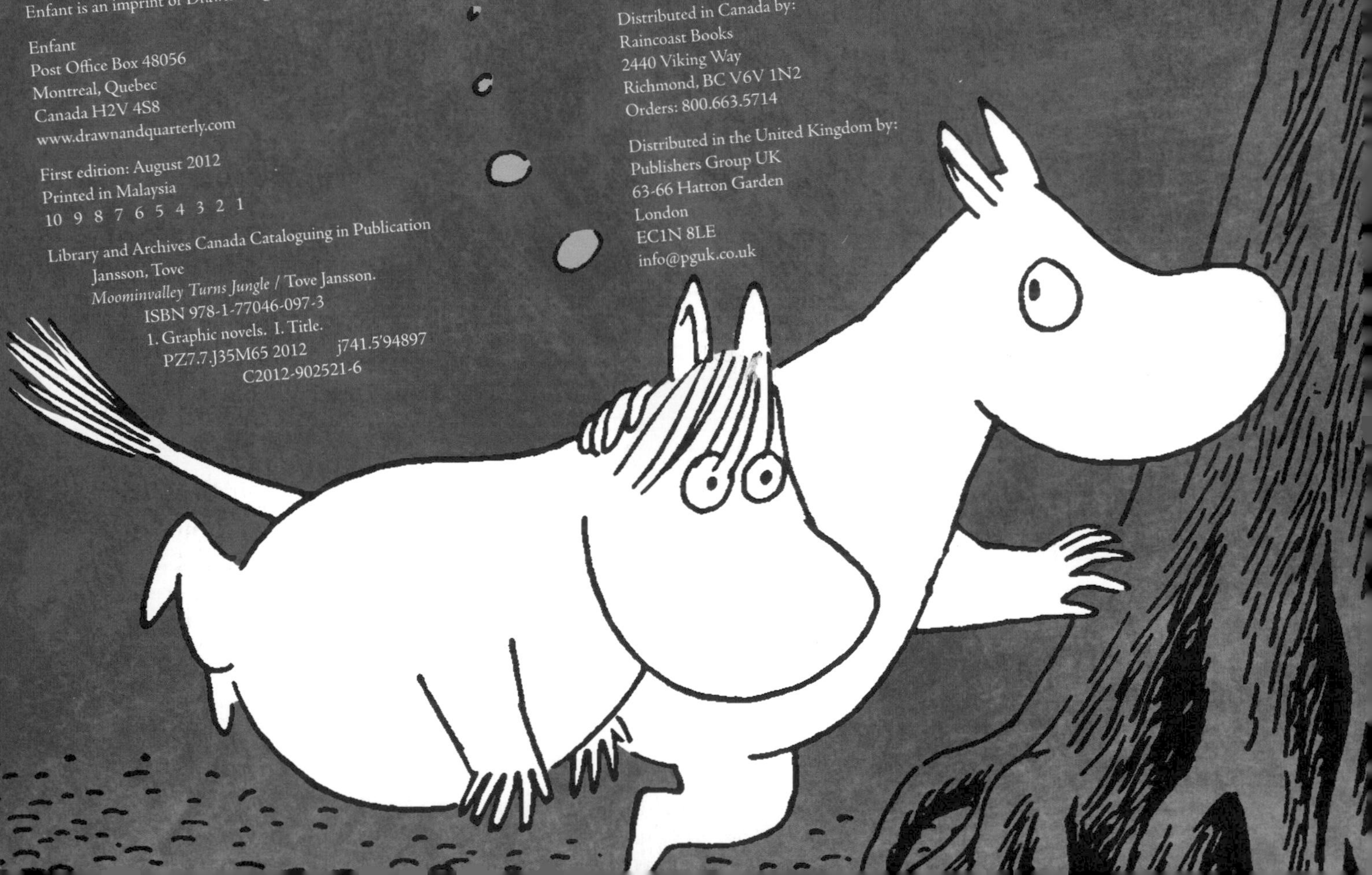

MOOMINVALLEY TURNS JUNGLE

Tove Jansson

ENFANT

MONTREAL

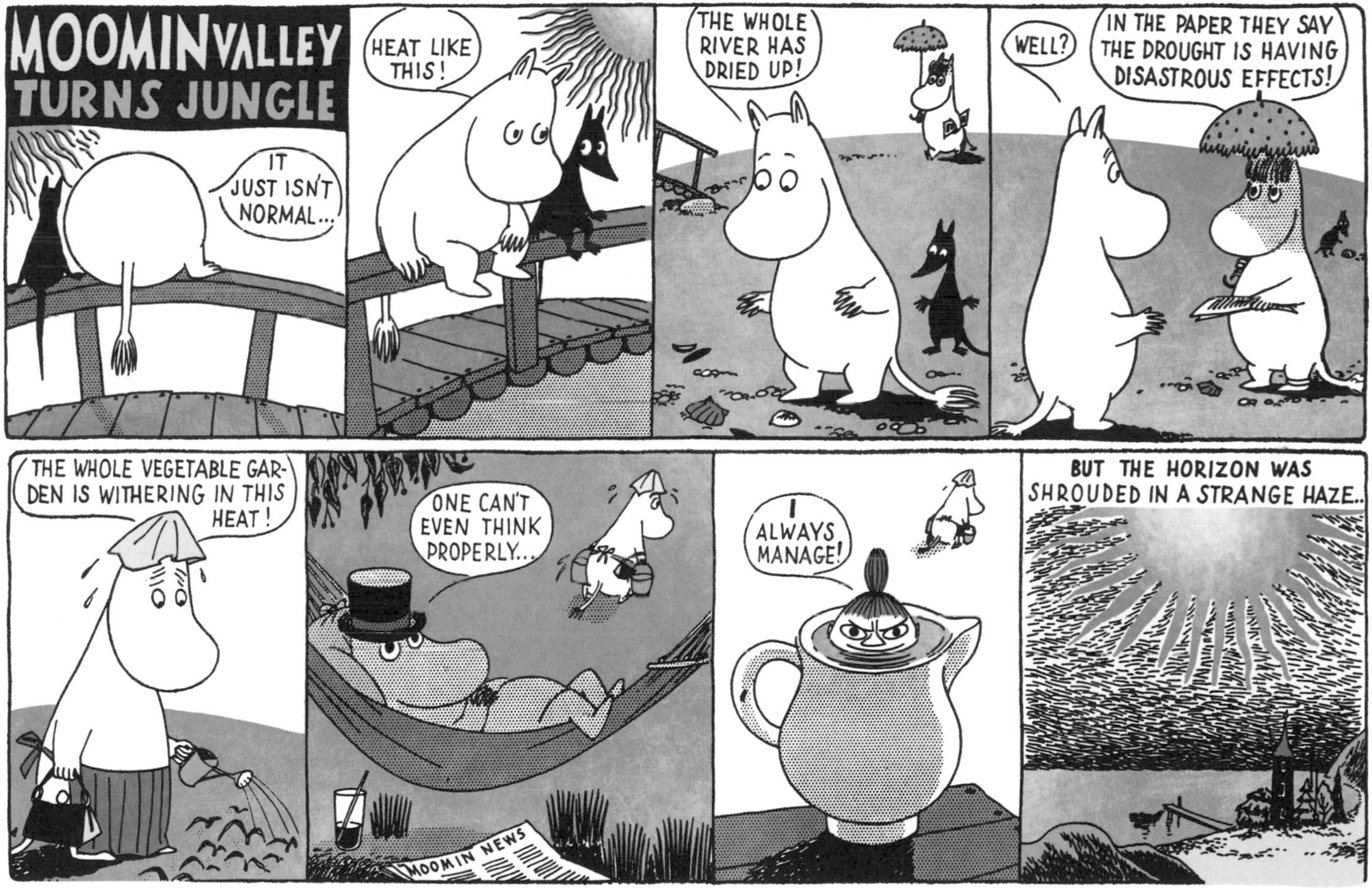
MOOMINVALLEY TURNS JUNGLE
IT JUST ISN'T NORMAL...
HEAT LIKE THIS!
THE WHOLE RIVER HAS DRIED UP!
WELL?
IN THE PAPER THEY SAY THE DROUGHT IS HAVING DISASTROUS EFFECTS!
THE WHOLE VEGETABLE GARDEN IS WITHERING IN THIS HEAT!
ONE CAN'T EVEN THINK PROPERLY...
MOOMIN NEWS
I ALWAYS MANAGE!
BUT THE HORIZON WAS SHROUDED IN A STRANGE HAZE..

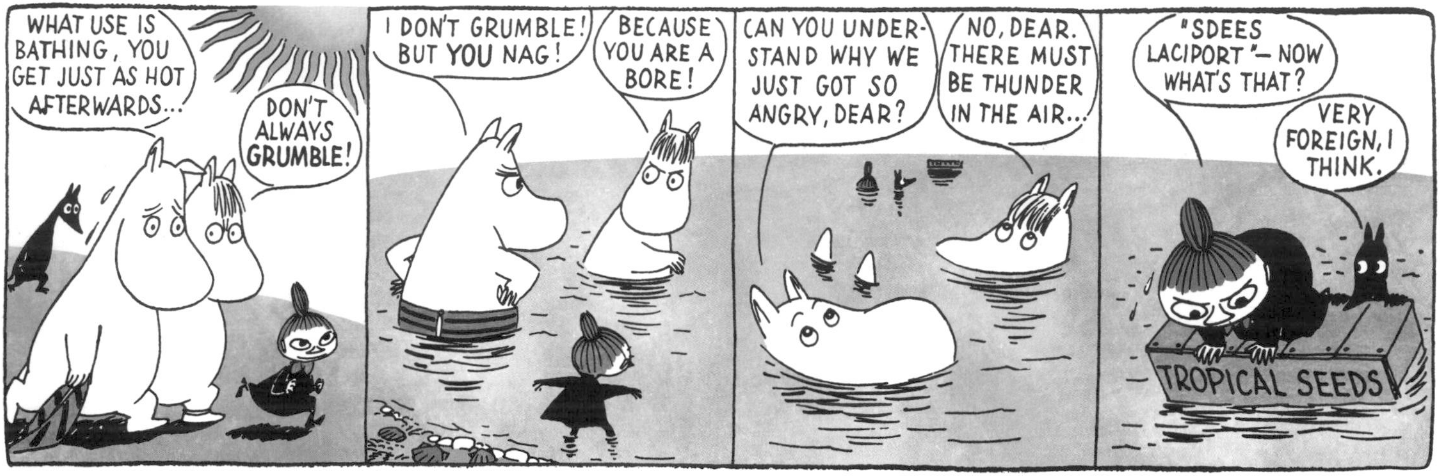
WHAT USE IS BATHING, YOU GET JUST AS HOT AFTERWARDS...
DON'T ALWAYS GRUMBLE!
I DON'T GRUMBLE! BUT YOU NAG!
BECAUSE YOU ARE A BORE!
CAN YOU UNDERSTAND WHY WE JUST GOT SO ANGRY, DEAR?
NO, DEAR. THERE MUST BE THUNDER IN THE AIR...
"SDEES LACIPORT"— NOW WHAT'S THAT?
VERY FOREIGN, I THINK.
TROPICAL SEEDS

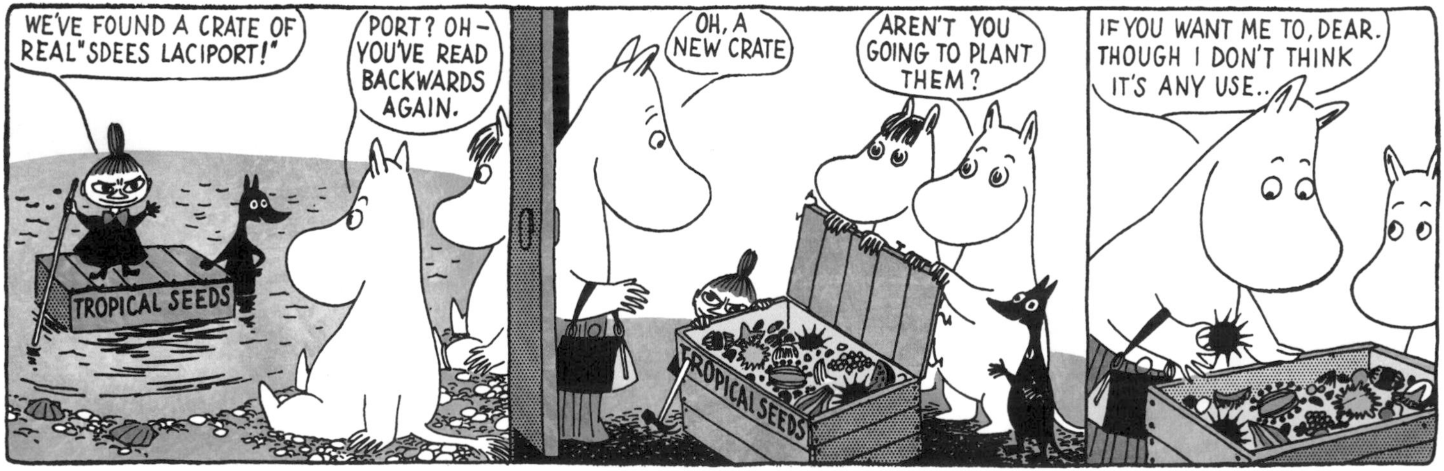
WE'VE FOUND A CRATE OF REAL "SDEES LACIPORT!"
PORT? OH— YOU'VE READ BACKWARDS AGAIN.
TROPICAL SEEDS
OH, A NEW CRATE
AREN'T YOU GOING TO PLANT THEM?
TROPICAL SEEDS
IF YOU WANT ME TO, DEAR. THOUGH I DON'T THINK IT'S ANY USE..

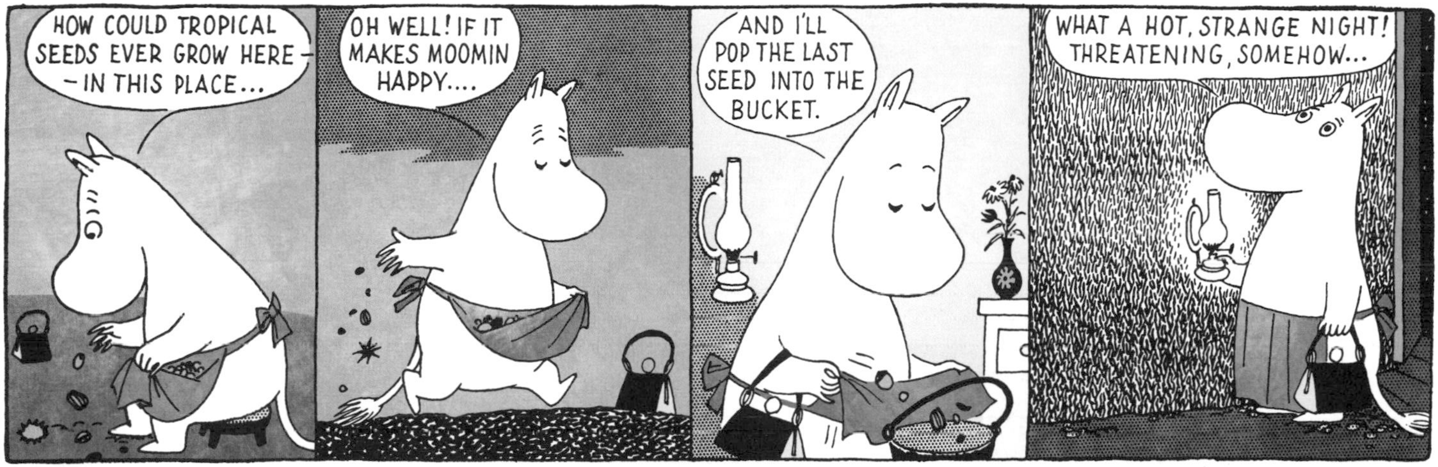
HOW COULD TROPICAL SEEDS EVER GROW HERE—IN THIS PLACE...
OH WELL! IF IT MAKES MOOMIN HAPPY....
AND I'LL POP THE LAST SEED INTO THE BUCKET.
WHAT A HOT, STRANGE NIGHT! THREATENING, SOMEHOW...

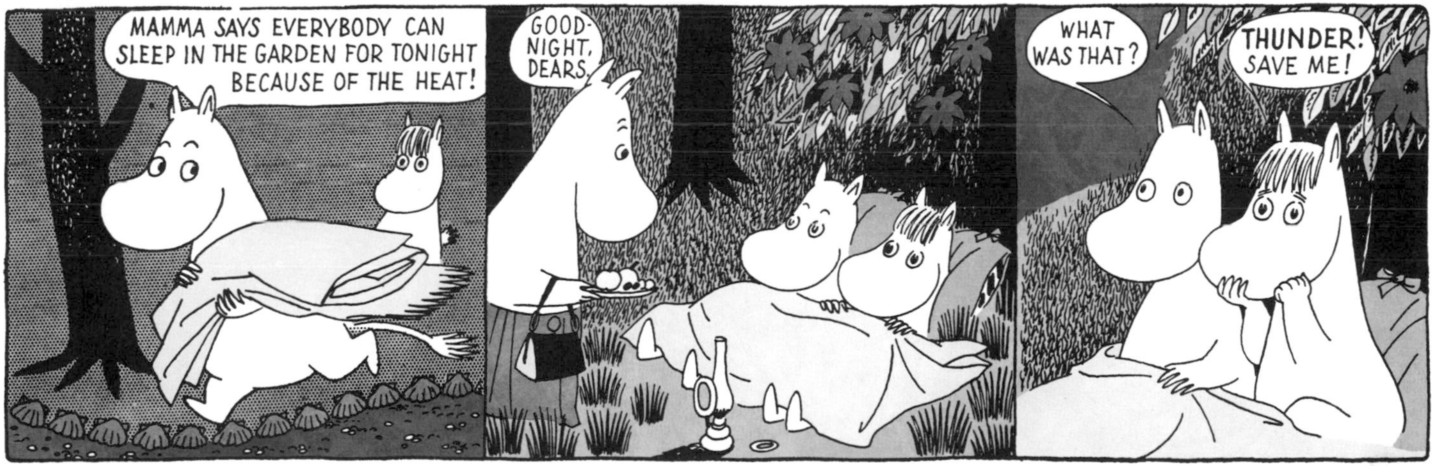
MAMMA SAYS EVERYBODY CAN SLEEP IN THE GARDEN FOR TONIGHT BECAUSE OF THE HEAT!
GOOD-NIGHT, DEARS.
WHAT WAS THAT?
THUNDER! SAVE ME!

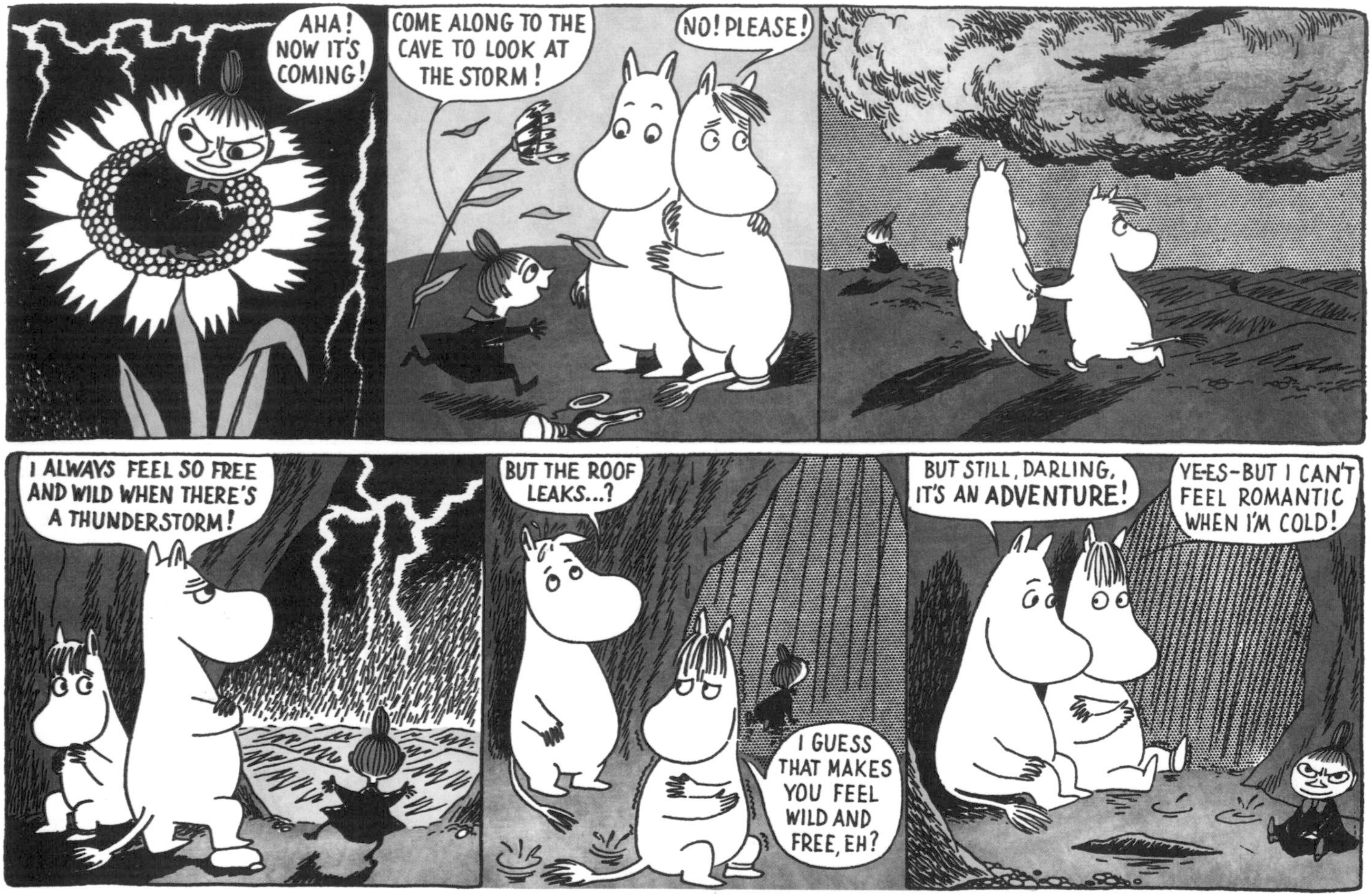
AHA! NOW IT'S COMING!
COME ALONG TO THE CAVE TO LOOK AT THE STORM!
NO! PLEASE!
I ALWAYS FEEL SO FREE AND WILD WHEN THERE'S A THUNDERSTORM!
BUT THE ROOF LEAKS...?
I GUESS THAT MAKES YOU FEEL WILD AND FREE, EH?
BUT STILL, DARLING, IT'S AN ADVENTURE!
YE-ES–BUT I CAN'T FEEL ROMANTIC WHEN I'M COLD!

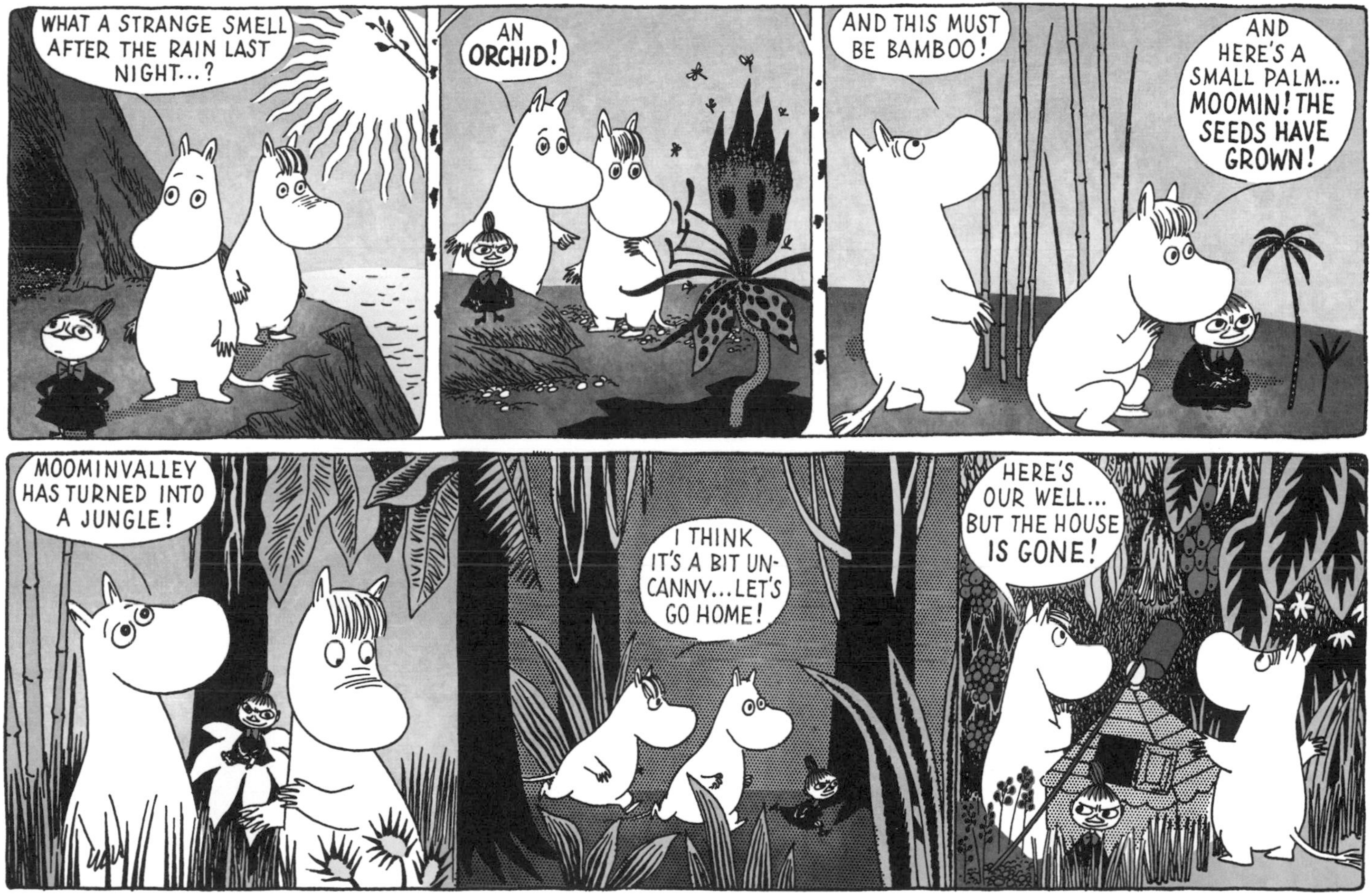
WHAT A STRANGE SMELL AFTER THE RAIN LAST NIGHT...?
AN ORCHID!
AND THIS MUST BE BAMBOO!
AND HERE'S A SMALL PALM... MOOMIN! THE SEEDS HAVE GROWN!
MOOMINVALLEY HAS TURNED INTO A JUNGLE!
I THINK IT'S A BIT UN-CANNY...LET'S GO HOME!
HERE'S OUR WELL... BUT THE HOUSE IS GONE!

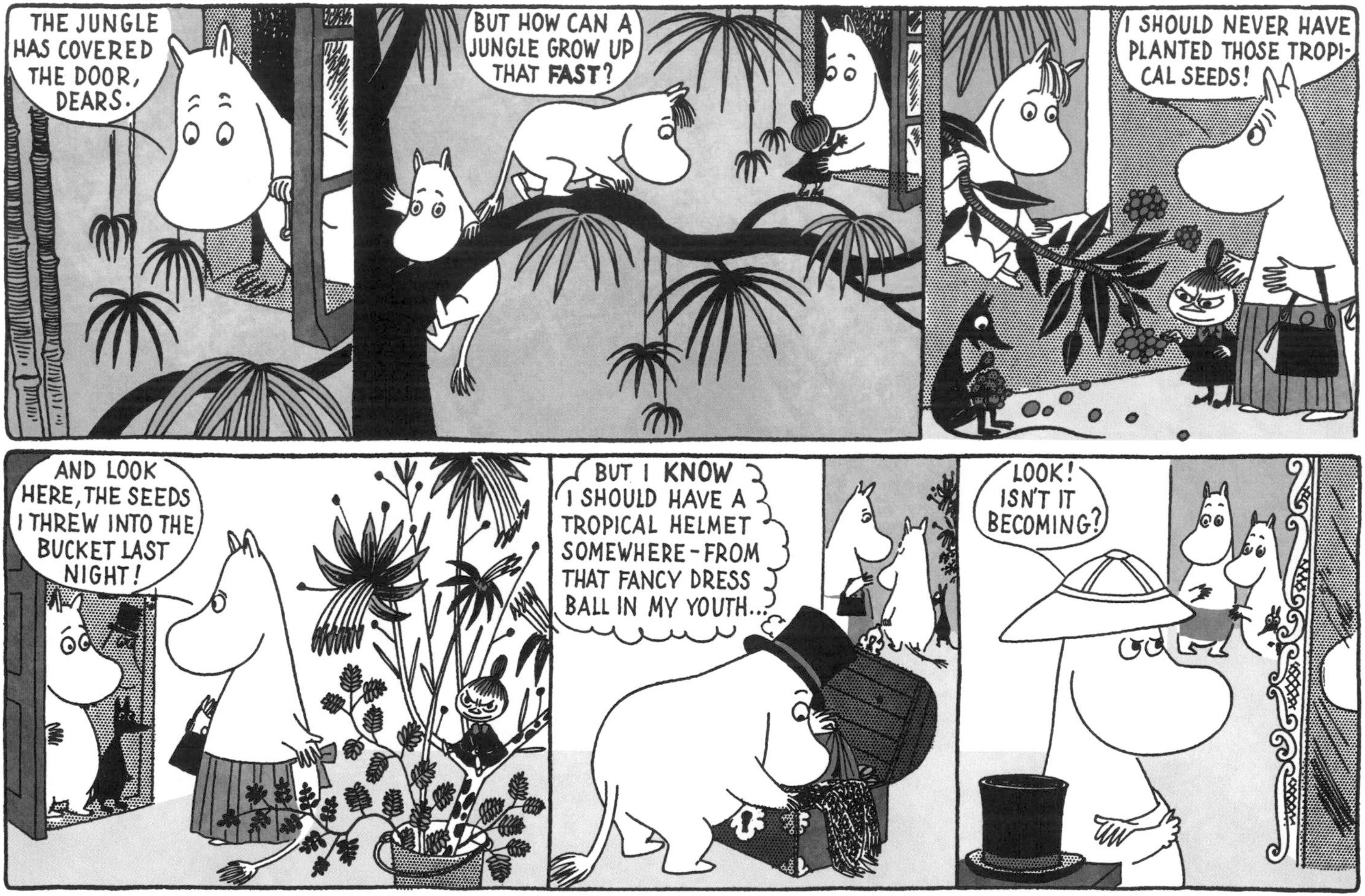
THE JUNGLE HAS COVERED THE DOOR, DEARS.
BUT HOW CAN A JUNGLE GROW UP THAT **FAST**?
I SHOULD NEVER HAVE PLANTED THOSE TROPICAL SEEDS!
AND LOOK HERE, THE SEEDS I THREW INTO THE BUCKET LAST NIGHT!
BUT I **KNOW** I SHOULD HAVE A TROPICAL HELMET SOMEWHERE – FROM THAT FANCY DRESS BALL IN MY YOUTH...
LOOK! ISN'T IT BECOMING?

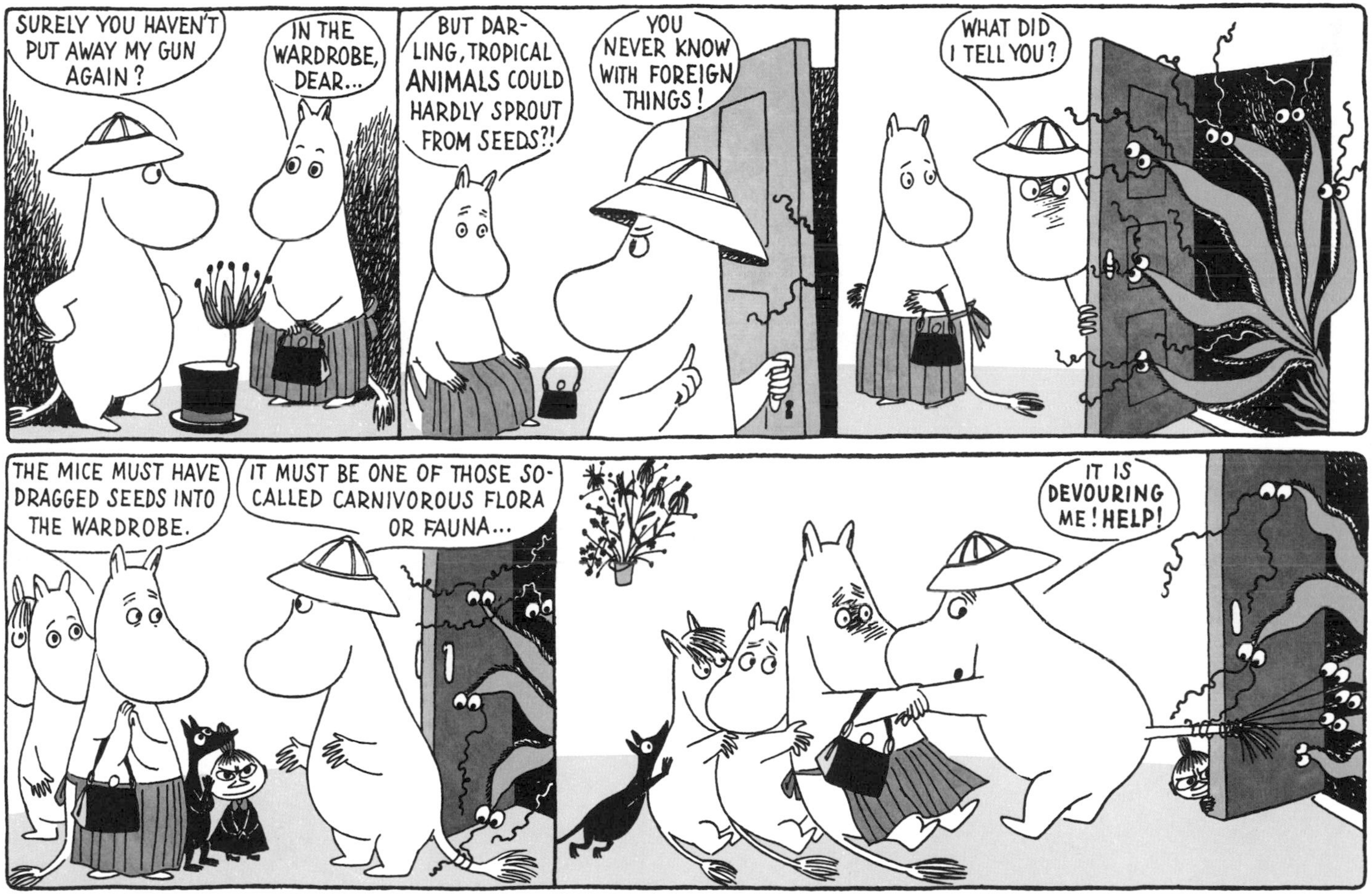
SURELY YOU HAVEN'T PUT AWAY MY GUN AGAIN?
IN THE WARDROBE, DEAR...
BUT DARLING, TROPICAL ANIMALS COULD HARDLY SPROUT FROM SEEDS?!
YOU NEVER KNOW WITH FOREIGN THINGS!
WHAT DID I TELL YOU?
THE MICE MUST HAVE DRAGGED SEEDS INTO THE WARDROBE.
IT MUST BE ONE OF THOSE SO-CALLED CARNIVOROUS FLORA OR FAUNA...
IT IS DEVOURING ME! HELP!

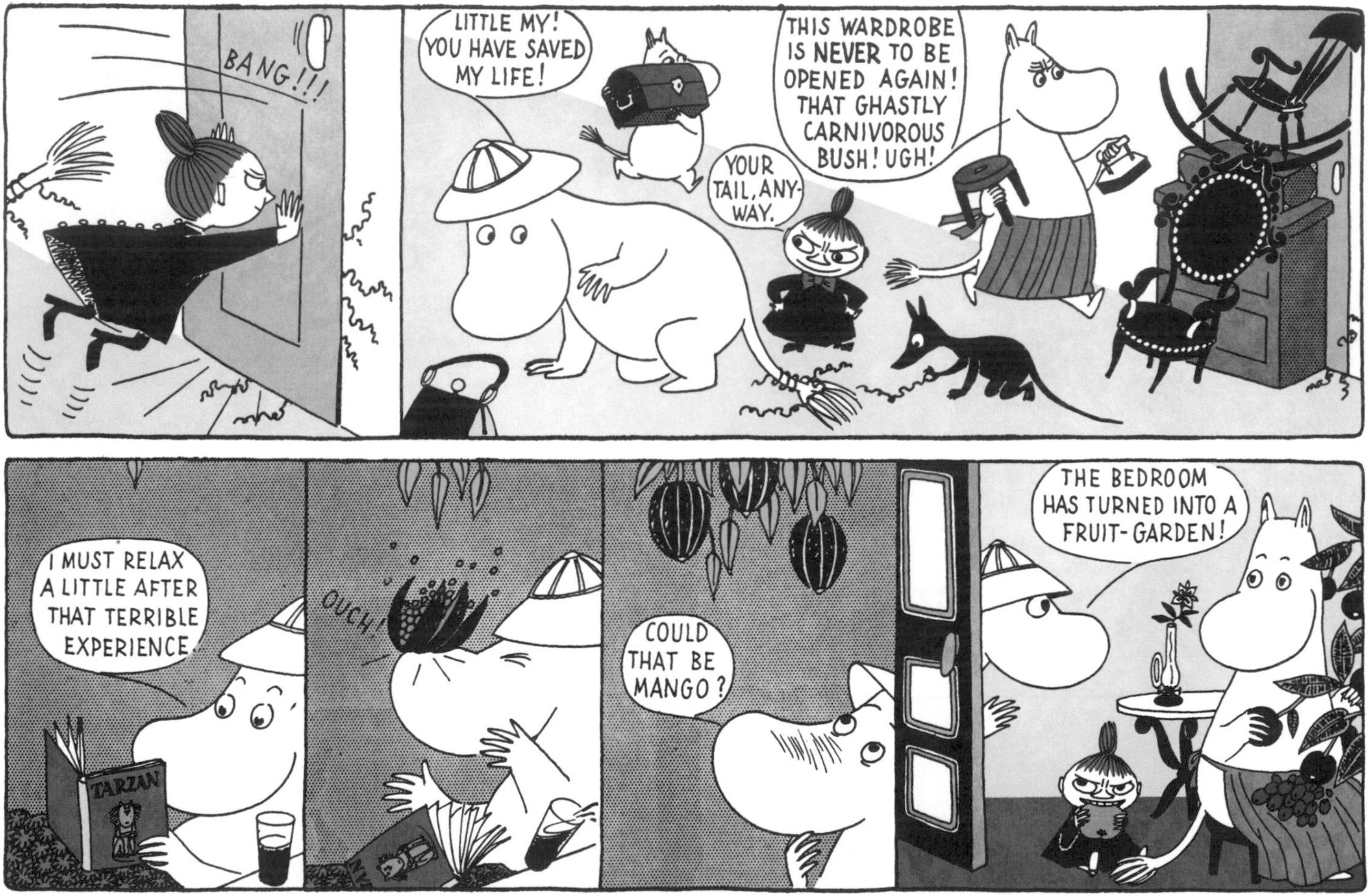
BANG!!!
LITTLE MY! YOU HAVE SAVED MY LIFE!
YOUR TAIL, ANYWAY.
THIS WARDROBE IS NEVER TO BE OPENED AGAIN! THAT GHASTLY CARNIVOROUS BUSH! UGH!
I MUST RELAX A LITTLE AFTER THAT TERRIBLE EXPERIENCE.
TARZAN
OUCH!
COULD THAT BE MANGO?
THE BEDROOM HAS TURNED INTO A FRUIT-GARDEN!

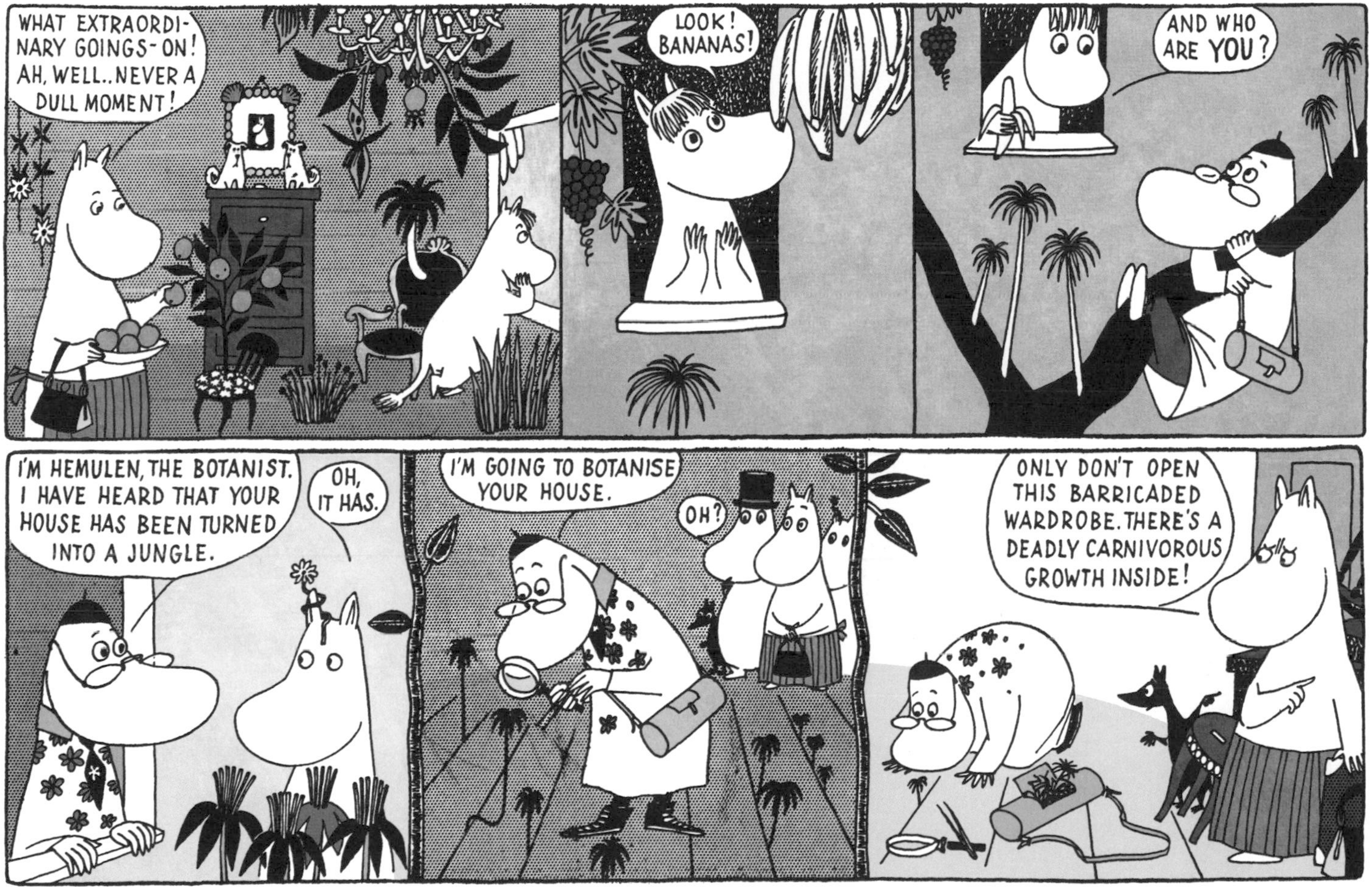
WHAT EXTRAORDI-NARY GOINGS-ON! AH, WELL..NEVER A DULL MOMENT!
LOOK! BANANAS!
AND WHO ARE YOU?
I'M HEMULEN, THE BOTANIST. I HAVE HEARD THAT YOUR HOUSE HAS BEEN TURNED INTO A JUNGLE.
OH, IT HAS.
I'M GOING TO BOTANISE YOUR HOUSE.
OH?
ONLY DON'T OPEN THIS BARRICADED WARDROBE. THERE'S A DEADLY CARNIVOROUS GROWTH INSIDE!

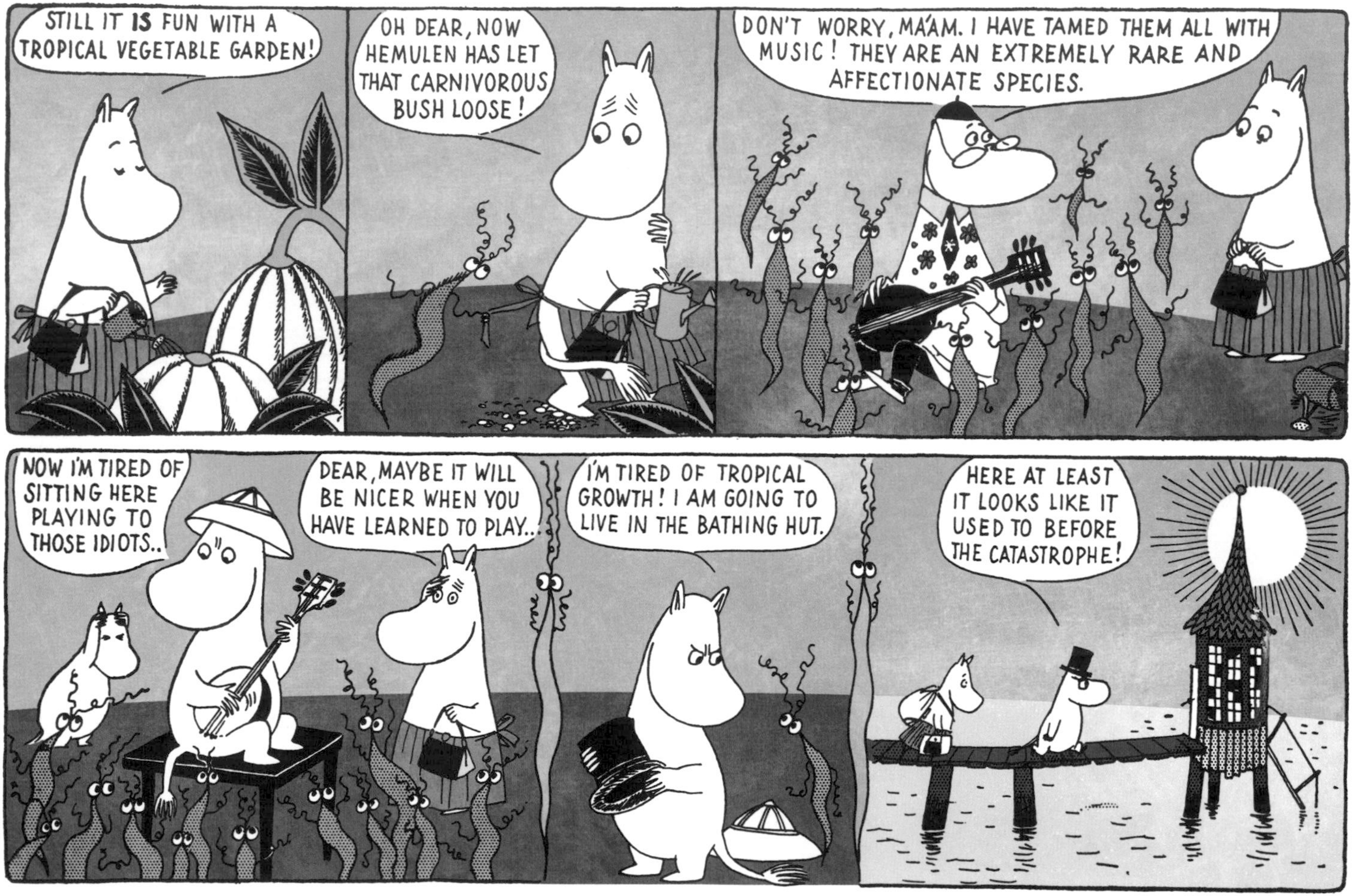
STILL IT IS FUN WITH A TROPICAL VEGETABLE GARDEN!
OH DEAR, NOW HEMULEN HAS LET THAT CARNIVOROUS BUSH LOOSE!
DON'T WORRY, MA'AM. I HAVE TAMED THEM ALL WITH MUSIC! THEY ARE AN EXTREMELY RARE AND AFFECTIONATE SPECIES.
NOW I'M TIRED OF SITTING HERE PLAYING TO THOSE IDIOTS..
DEAR, MAYBE IT WILL BE NICER WHEN YOU HAVE LEARNED TO PLAY..
I'M TIRED OF TROPICAL GROWTH! I AM GOING TO LIVE IN THE BATHING HUT.
HERE AT LEAST IT LOOKS LIKE IT USED TO BEFORE THE CATASTROPHE!

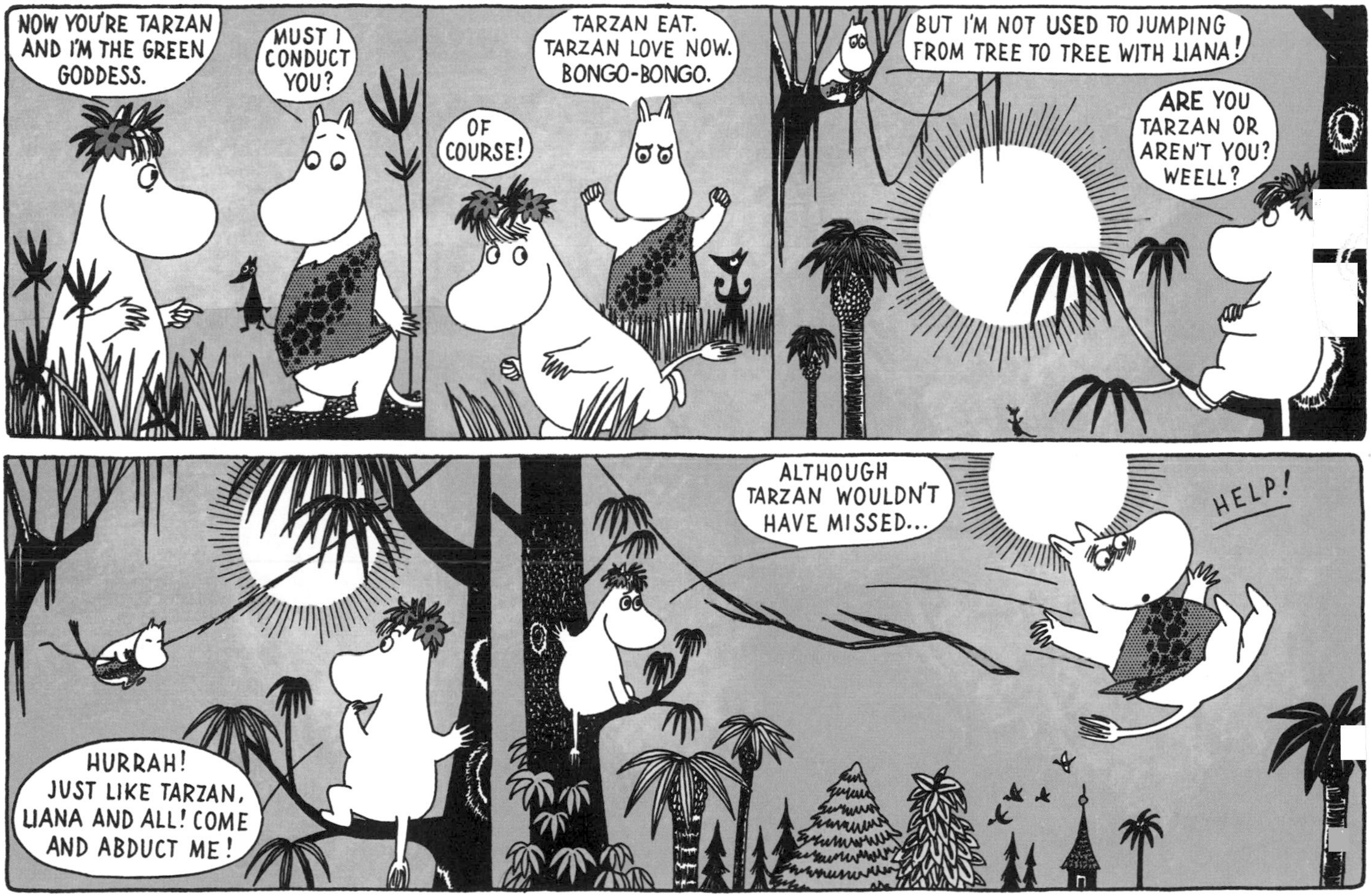
NOW YOU'RE TARZAN AND I'M THE GREEN GODDESS.
MUST I CONDUCT YOU?
TARZAN EAT. TARZAN LOVE NOW. BONGO-BONGO.
OF COURSE!
BUT I'M NOT USED TO JUMPING FROM TREE TO TREE WITH LIANA!
ARE YOU TARZAN OR AREN'T YOU? WEELL?
HURRAH! JUST LIKE TARZAN, LIANA AND ALL! COME AND ABDUCT ME!
ALTHOUGH TARZAN WOULDN'T HAVE MISSED...
HELP!

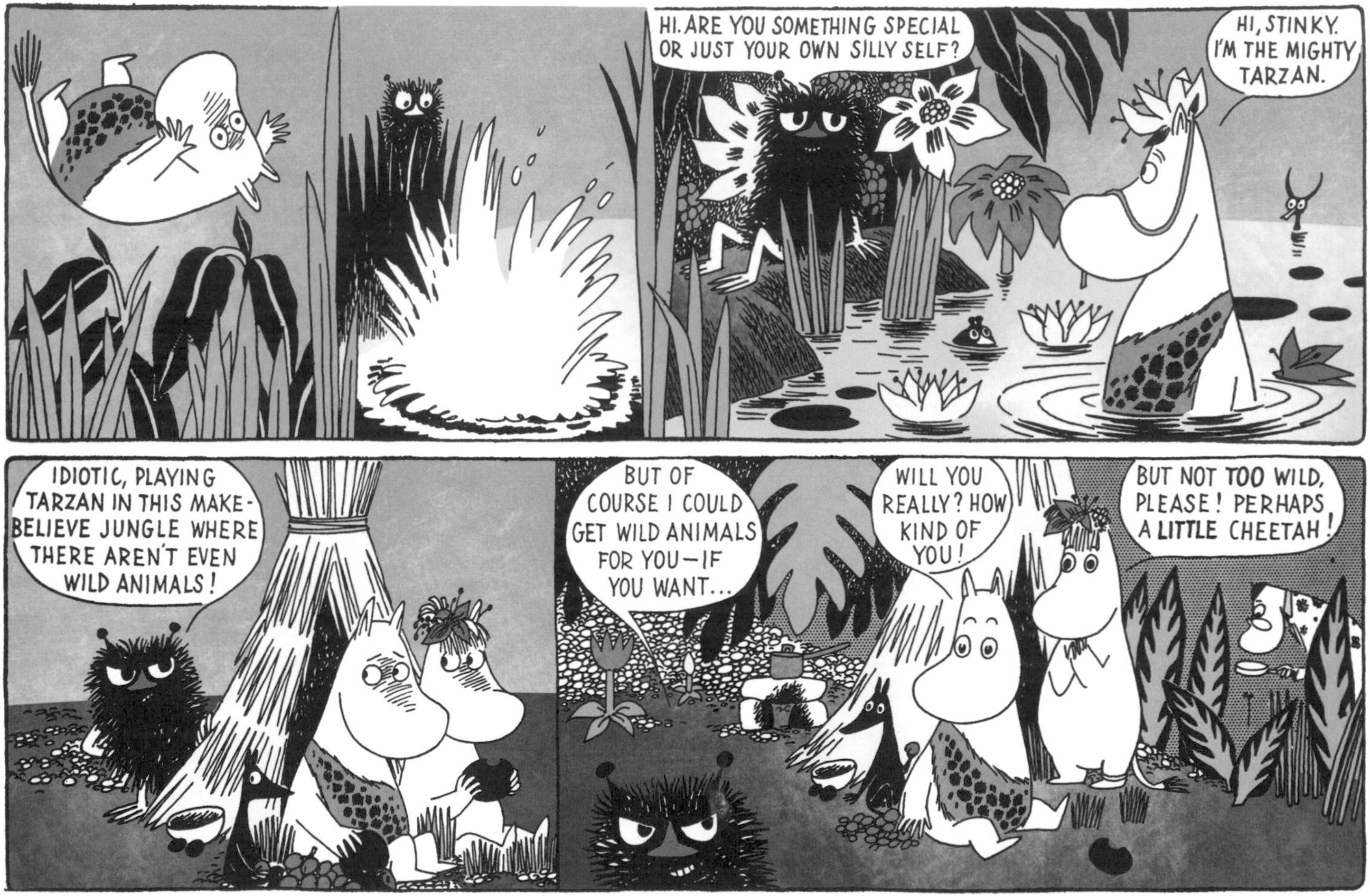
HI. ARE YOU SOMETHING SPECIAL OR JUST YOUR OWN SILLY SELF?
HI, STINKY. I'M THE MIGHTY TARZAN.
IDIOTIC, PLAYING TARZAN IN THIS MAKE-BELIEVE JUNGLE WHERE THERE AREN'T EVEN WILD ANIMALS!
BUT OF COURSE I COULD GET WILD ANIMALS FOR YOU – IF YOU WANT...
WILL YOU REALLY? HOW KIND OF YOU!
BUT NOT TOO WILD, PLEASE! PERHAPS A LITTLE CHEETAH!

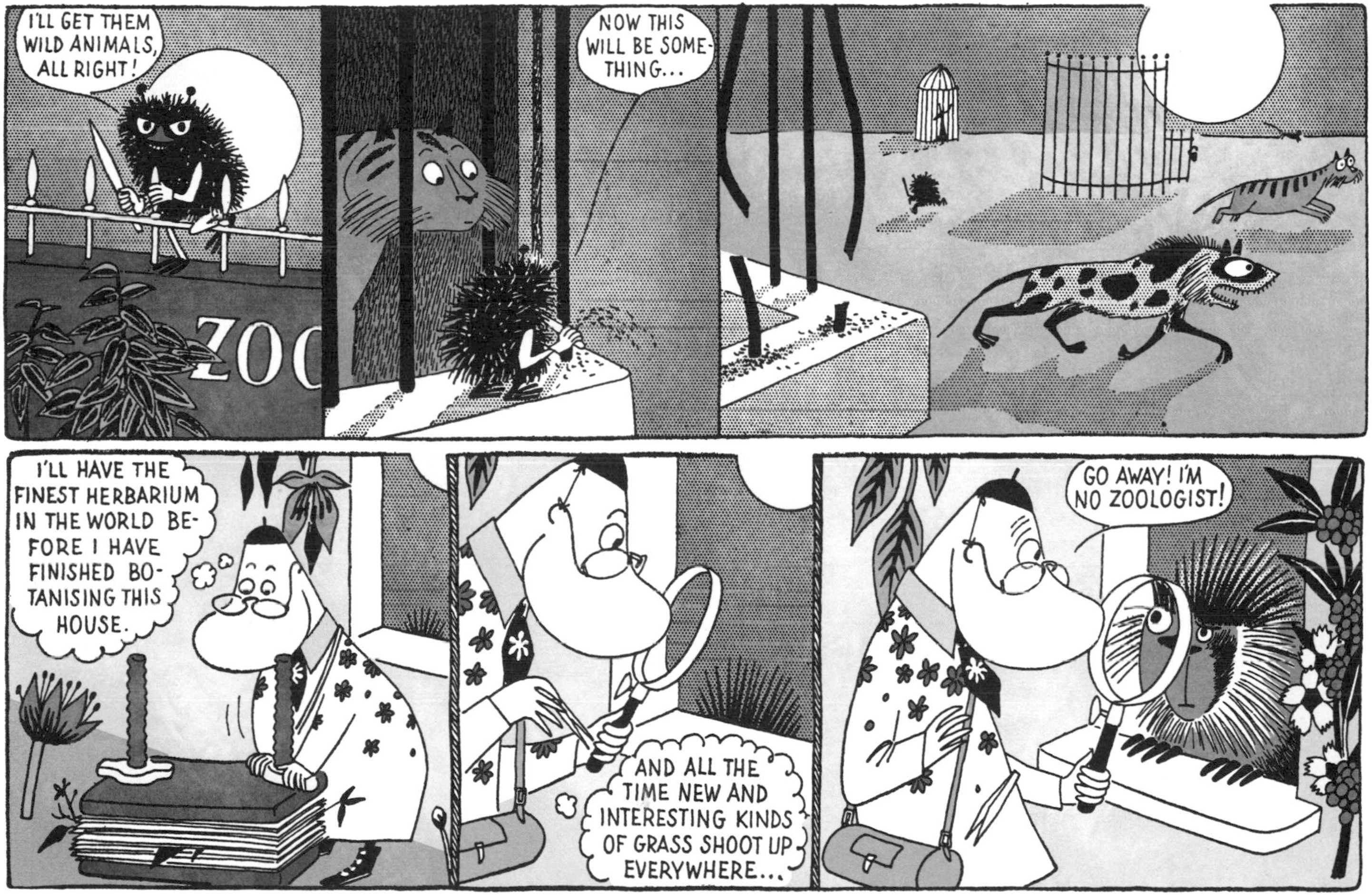

I'LL GET THEM WILD ANIMALS, ALL RIGHT!
ZOO
NOW THIS WILL BE SOME-THING...
I'LL HAVE THE FINEST HERBARIUM IN THE WORLD BE-FORE I HAVE FINISHED BO-TANISING THIS HOUSE.
AND ALL THE TIME NEW AND INTERESTING KINDS OF GRASS SHOOT UP EVERYWHERE...
GO AWAY! I'M NO ZOOLOGIST!

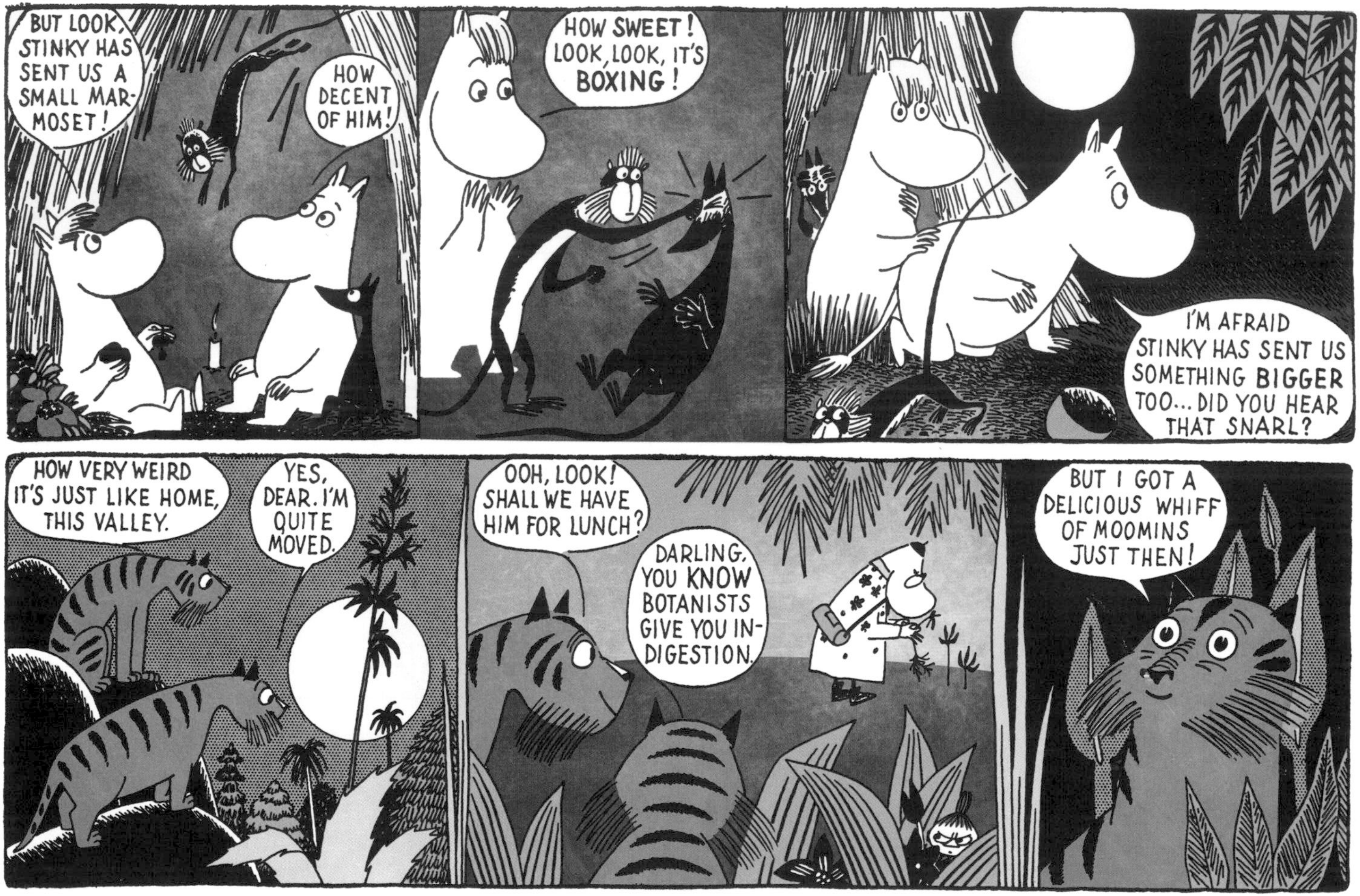
BUT LOOK, STINKY HAS SENT US A SMALL MAR-MOSET!
HOW DECENT OF HIM!
HOW SWEET! LOOK, LOOK, IT'S BOXING!
I'M AFRAID STINKY HAS SENT US SOMETHING BIGGER TOO... DID YOU HEAR THAT SNARL?
HOW VERY WEIRD IT'S JUST LIKE HOME, THIS VALLEY.
YES, DEAR. I'M QUITE MOVED.
OOH, LOOK! SHALL WE HAVE HIM FOR LUNCH?
DARLING, YOU KNOW BOTANISTS GIVE YOU IN-DIGESTION.
BUT I GOT A DELICIOUS WHIFF OF MOOMINS JUST THEN!

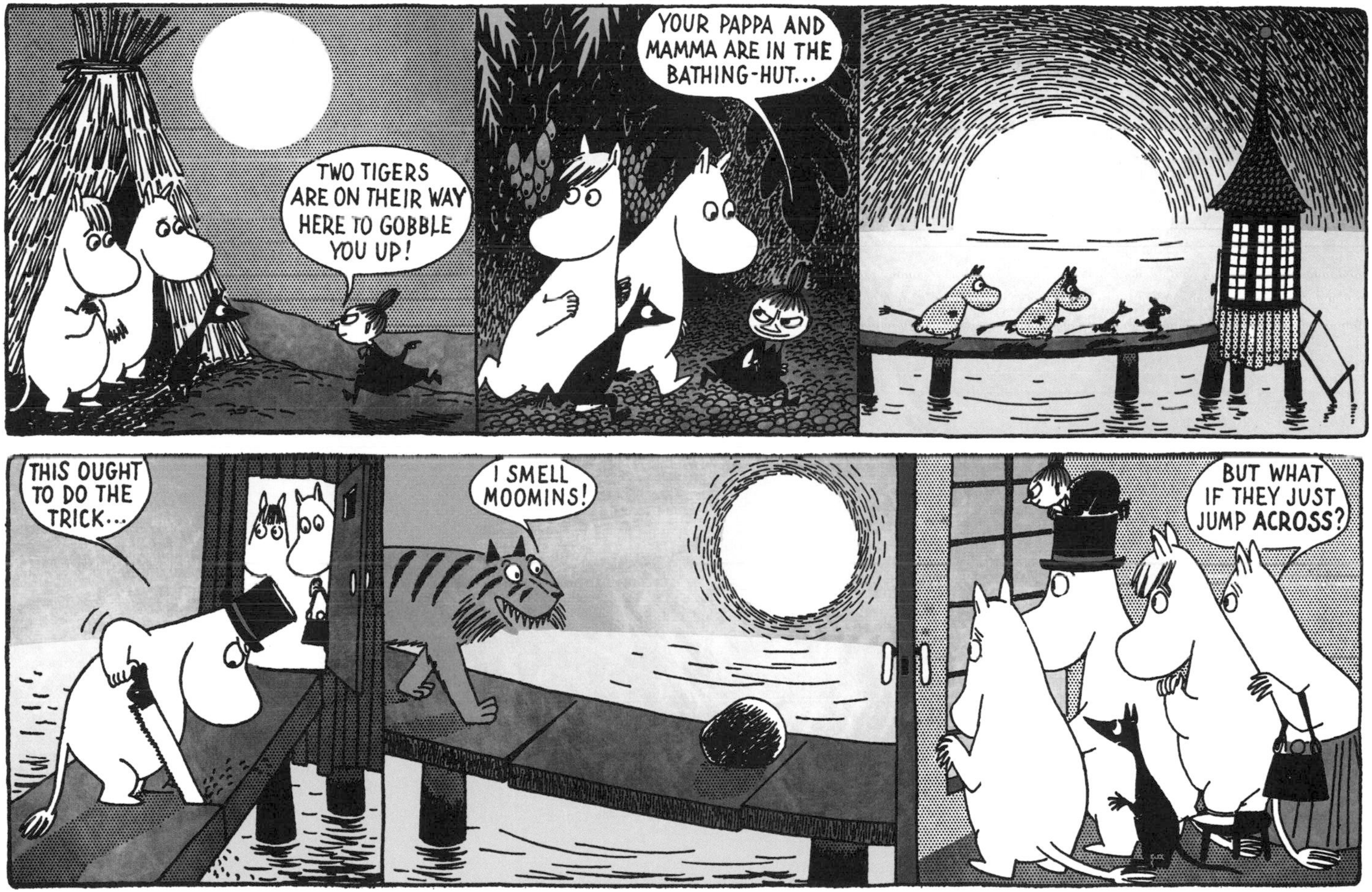
TWO TIGERS ARE ON THEIR WAY HERE TO GOBBLE YOU UP!
YOUR PAPPA AND MAMMA ARE IN THE BATHING-HUT...
THIS OUGHT TO DO THE TRICK...
I SMELL MOOMINS!
BUT WHAT IF THEY JUST JUMP ACROSS?

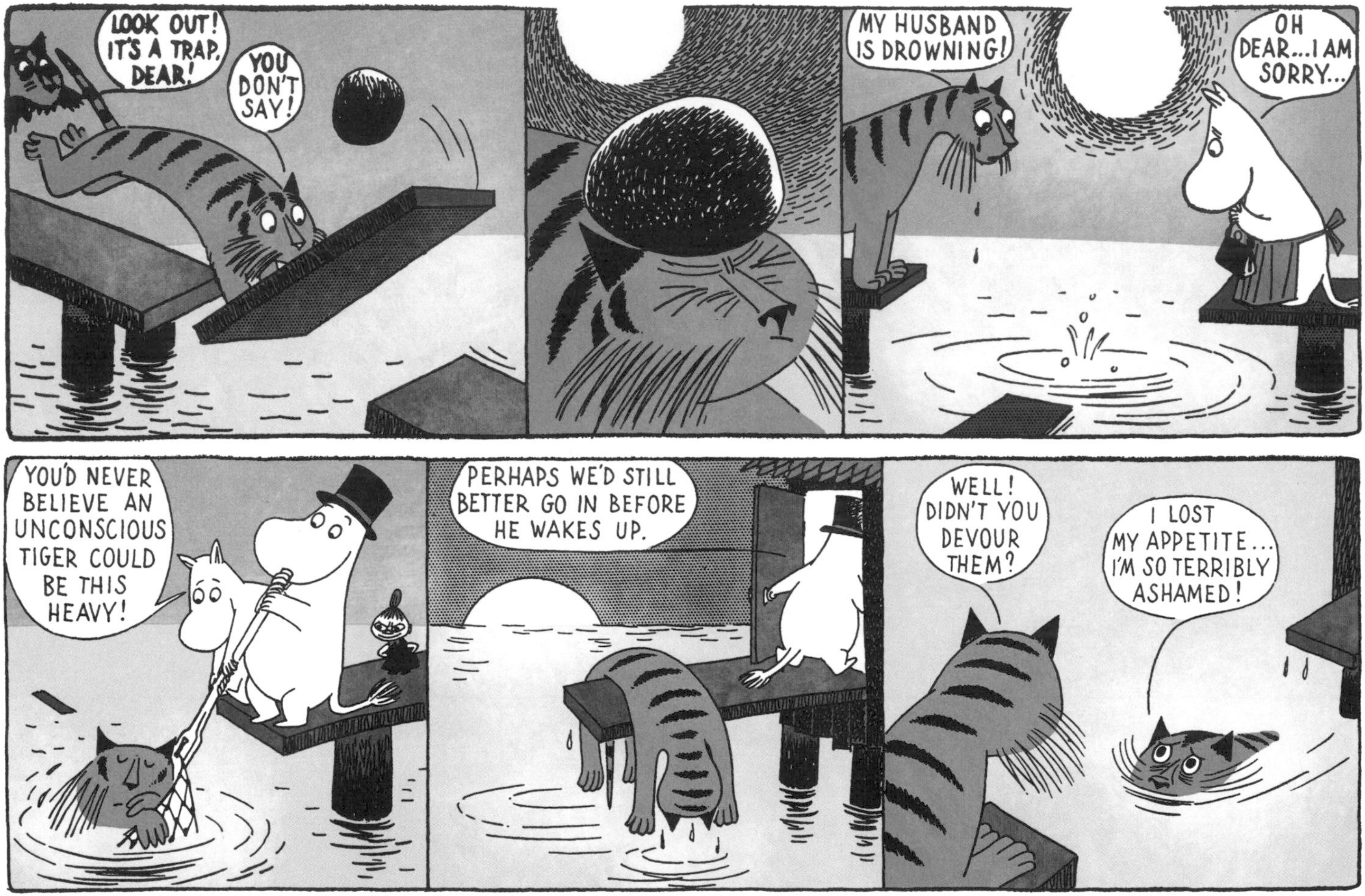
LOOK OUT! IT'S A TRAP, DEAR!
YOU DON'T SAY!
MY HUSBAND IS DROWNING!
OH DEAR...I AM SORRY...
YOU'D NEVER BELIEVE AN UNCONSCIOUS TIGER COULD BE THIS HEAVY!
PERHAPS WE'D STILL BETTER GO IN BEFORE HE WAKES UP.
WELL! DIDN'T YOU DEVOUR THEM?
I LOST MY APPETITE... I'M SO TERRIBLY ASHAMED!

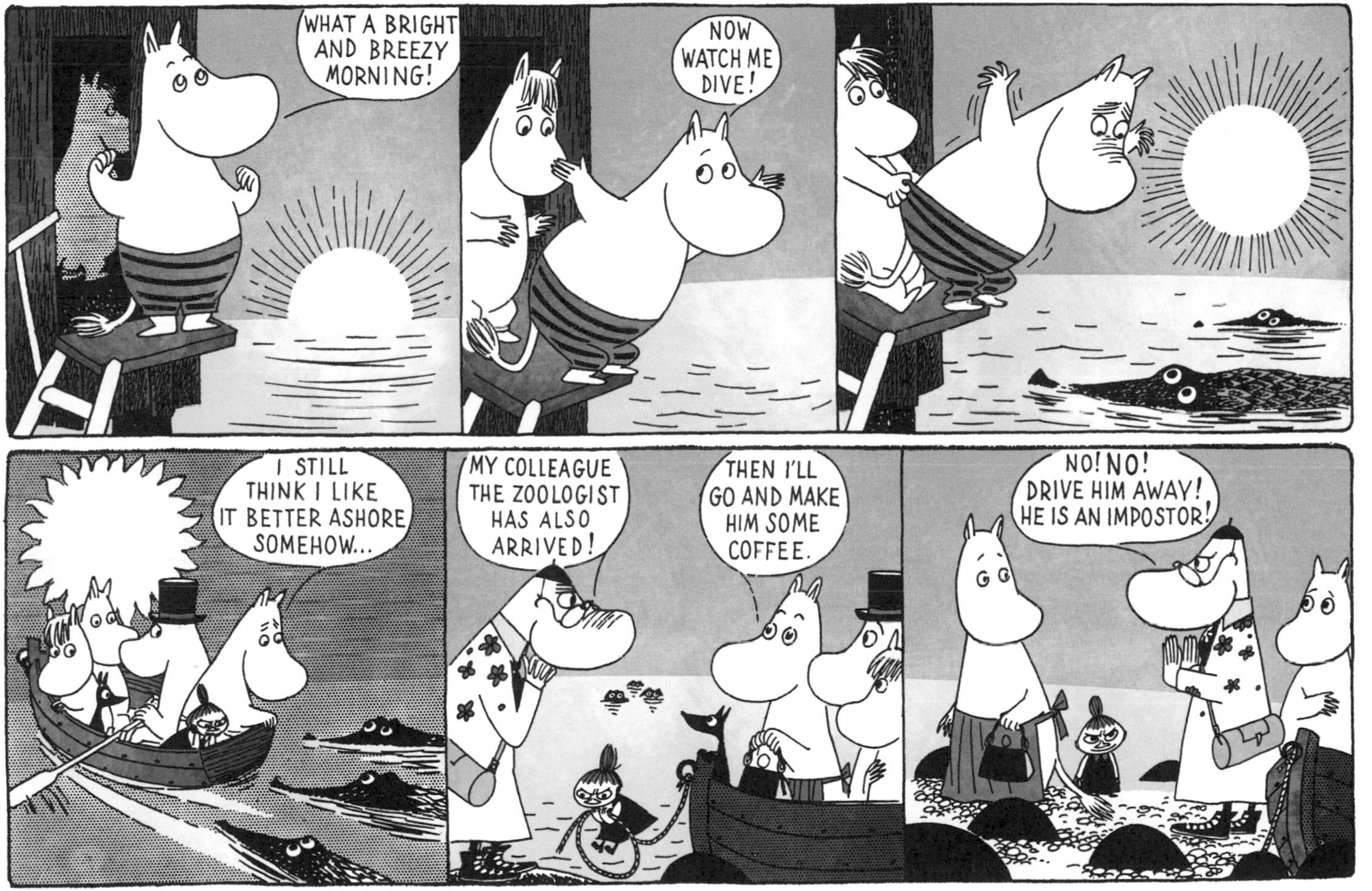
WHAT A BRIGHT AND BREEZY MORNING!
NOW WATCH ME DIVE!
I STILL THINK I LIKE IT BETTER ASHORE SOMEHOW...
MY COLLEAGUE THE ZOOLOGIST HAS ALSO ARRIVED!
THEN I'LL GO AND MAKE HIM SOME COFFEE.
NO! NO! DRIVE HIM AWAY! HE IS AN IMPOSTOR!

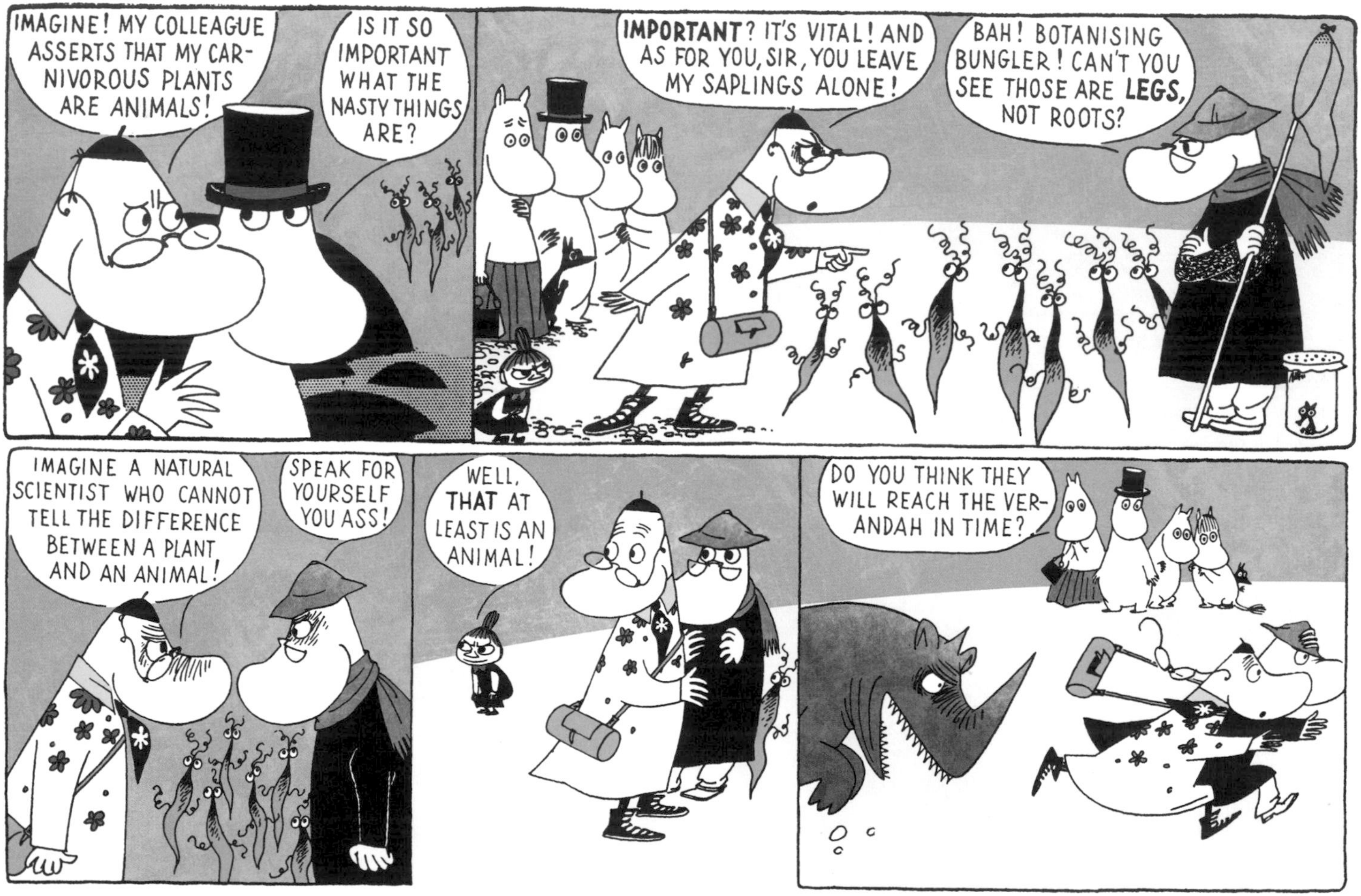
IMAGINE! MY COLLEAGUE ASSERTS THAT MY CAR-NIVOROUS PLANTS ARE ANIMALS!
IS IT SO IMPORTANT WHAT THE NASTY THINGS ARE?
IMPORTANT? IT'S VITAL! AND AS FOR YOU, SIR, YOU LEAVE MY SAPLINGS ALONE!
BAH! BOTANISING BUNGLER! CAN'T YOU SEE THOSE ARE **LEGS**, NOT ROOTS?
IMAGINE A NATURAL SCIENTIST WHO CANNOT TELL THE DIFFERENCE BETWEEN A PLANT AND AN ANIMAL!
SPEAK FOR YOURSELF YOU ASS!
WELL, **THAT** AT LEAST IS AN ANIMAL!
DO YOU THINK THEY WILL REACH THE VER-ANDAH IN TIME?

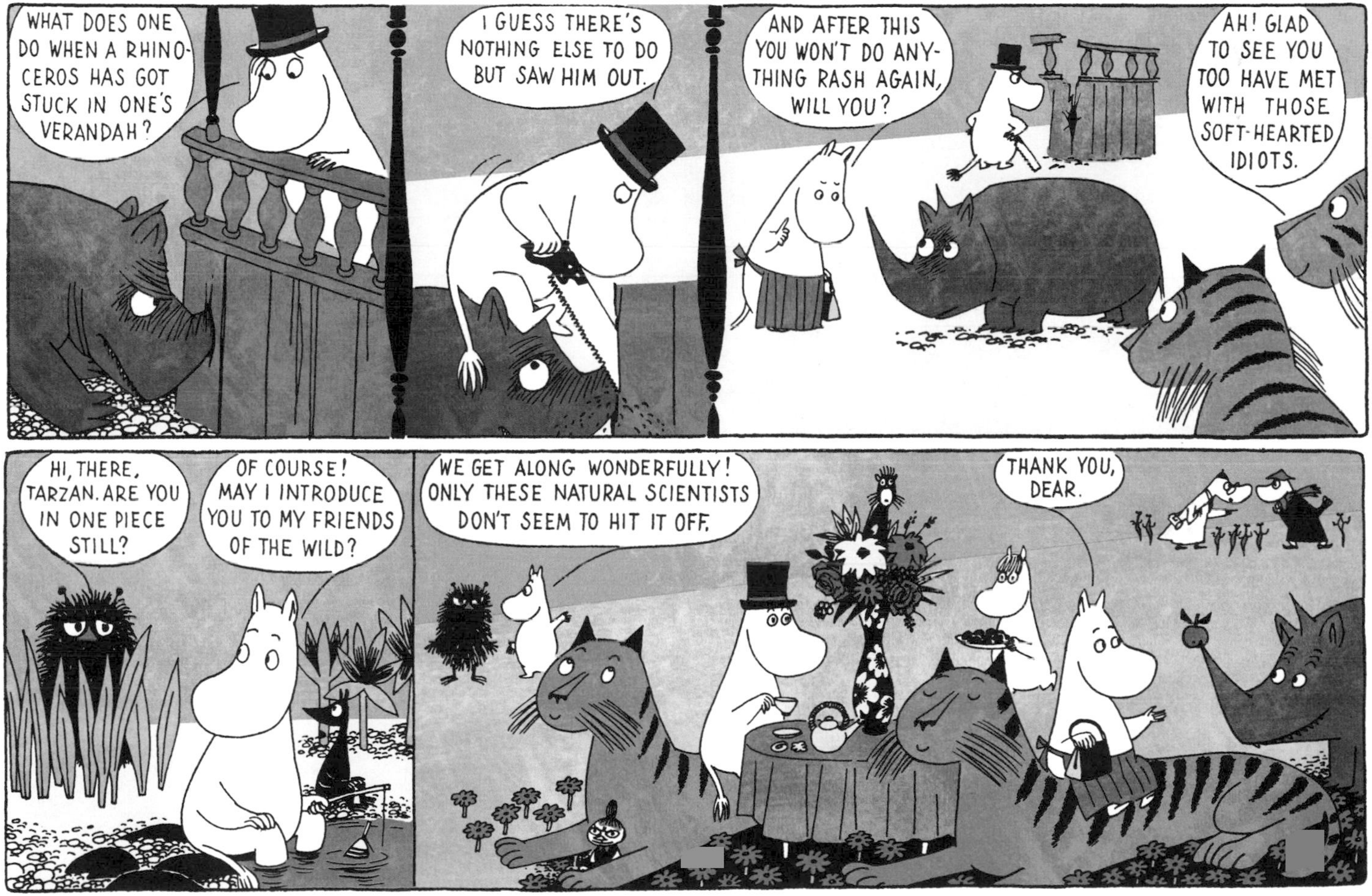
WHAT DOES ONE DO WHEN A RHINO-CEROS HAS GOT STUCK IN ONE'S VERANDAH?
I GUESS THERE'S NOTHING ELSE TO DO BUT SAW HIM OUT.
AND AFTER THIS YOU WON'T DO ANY-THING RASH AGAIN, WILL YOU?
AH! GLAD TO SEE YOU TOO HAVE MET WITH THOSE SOFT-HEARTED IDIOTS.
HI, THERE, TARZAN. ARE YOU IN ONE PIECE STILL?
OF COURSE! MAY I INTRODUCE YOU TO MY FRIENDS OF THE WILD?
WE GET ALONG WONDERFULLY! ONLY THESE NATURAL SCIENTISTS DON'T SEEM TO HIT IT OFF.
THANK YOU, DEAR.

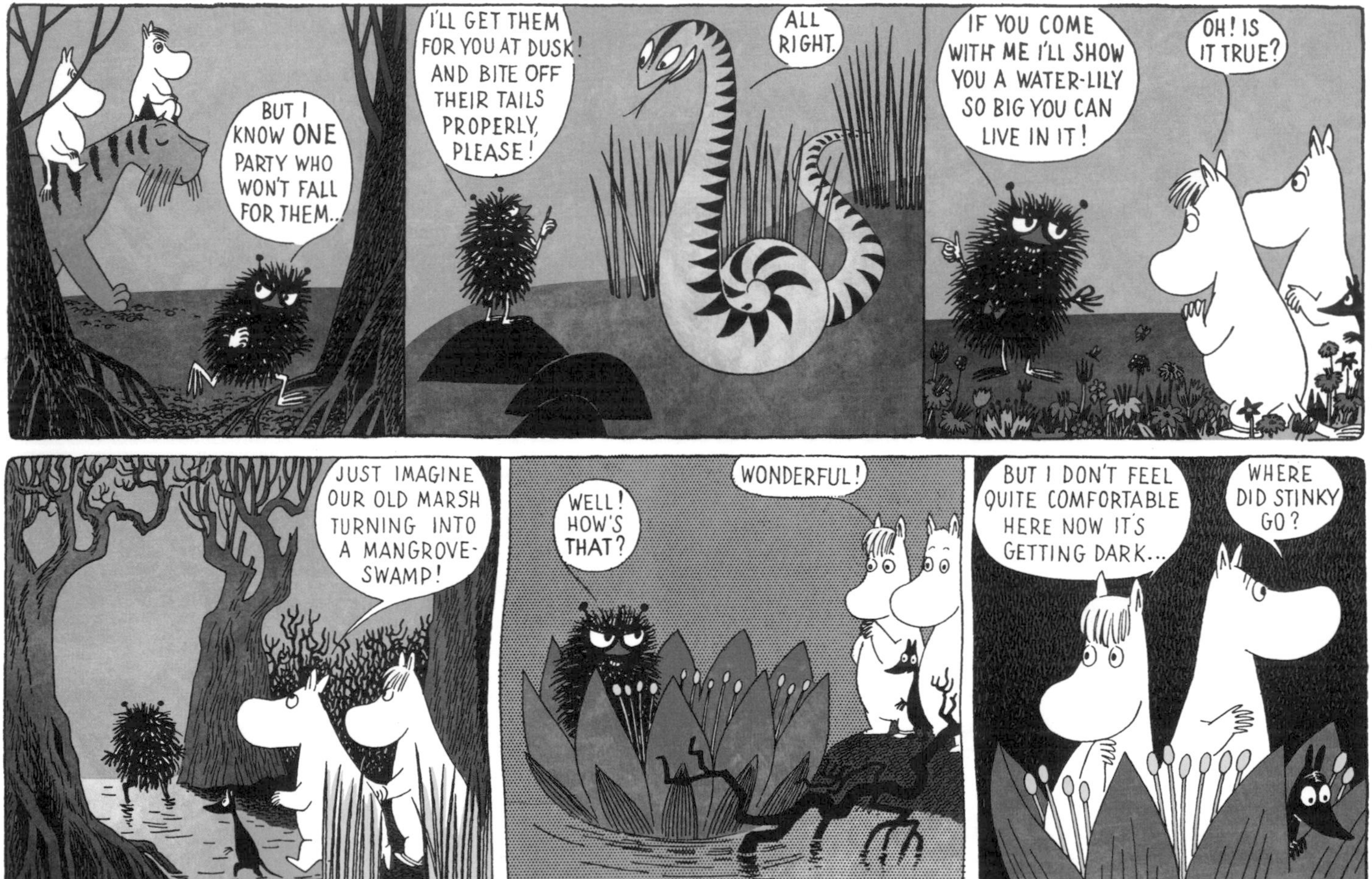
BUT I KNOW ONE PARTY WHO WON'T FALL FOR THEM...
I'LL GET THEM FOR YOU AT DUSK! AND BITE OFF THEIR TAILS PROPERLY, PLEASE!
ALL RIGHT.
IF YOU COME WITH ME I'LL SHOW YOU A WATER-LILY SO BIG YOU CAN LIVE IN IT!
OH! IS IT TRUE?
JUST IMAGINE OUR OLD MARSH TURNING INTO A MANGROVE-SWAMP!
WELL! HOW'S THAT?
WONDERFUL!
BUT I DON'T FEEL QUITE COMFORTABLE HERE NOW IT'S GETTING DARK...
WHERE DID STINKY GO?

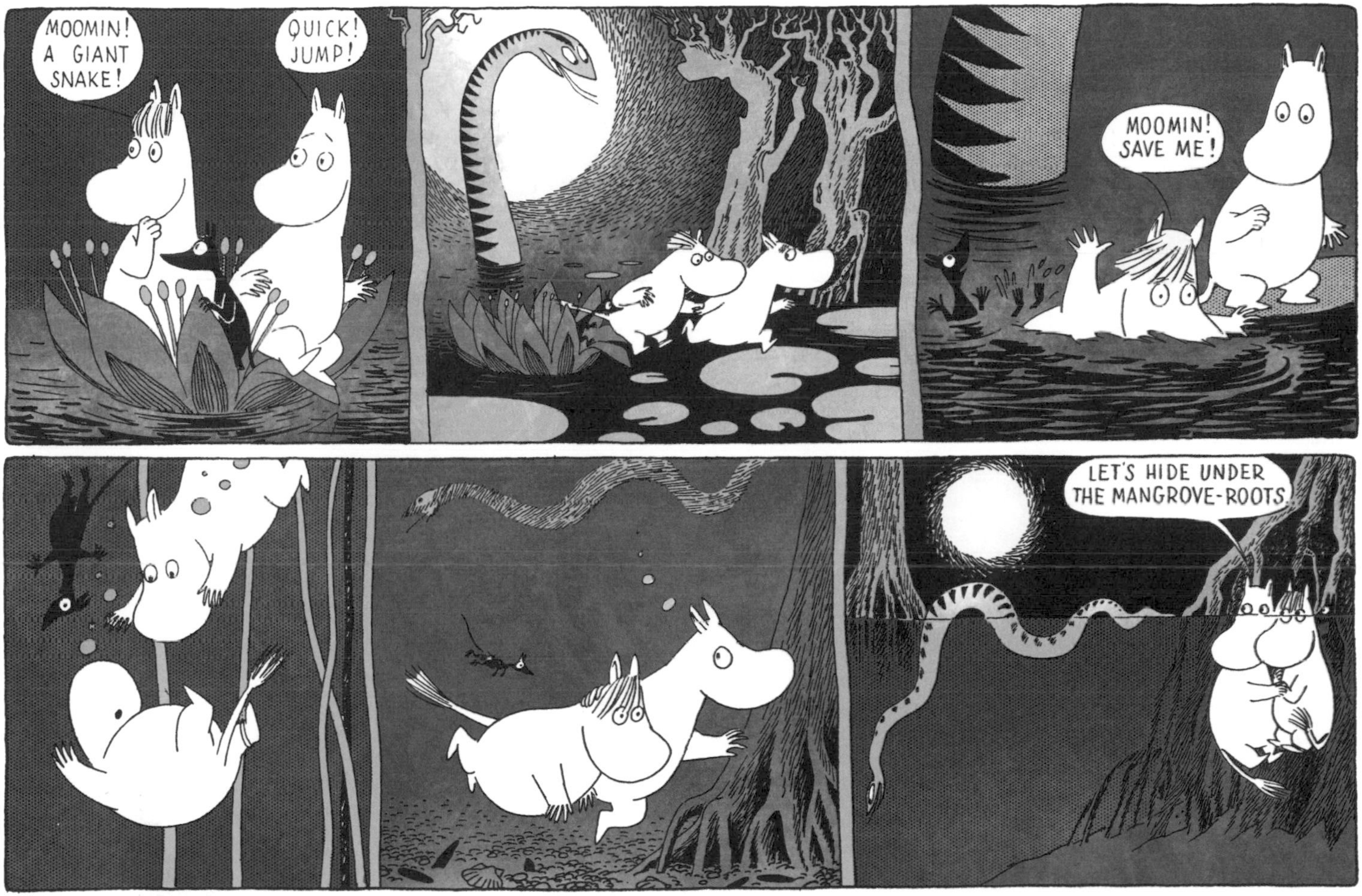
MOOMIN! A GIANT SNAKE!
QUICK! JUMP!
MOOMIN! SAVE ME!
LET'S HIDE UNDER THE MANGROVE-ROOTS.

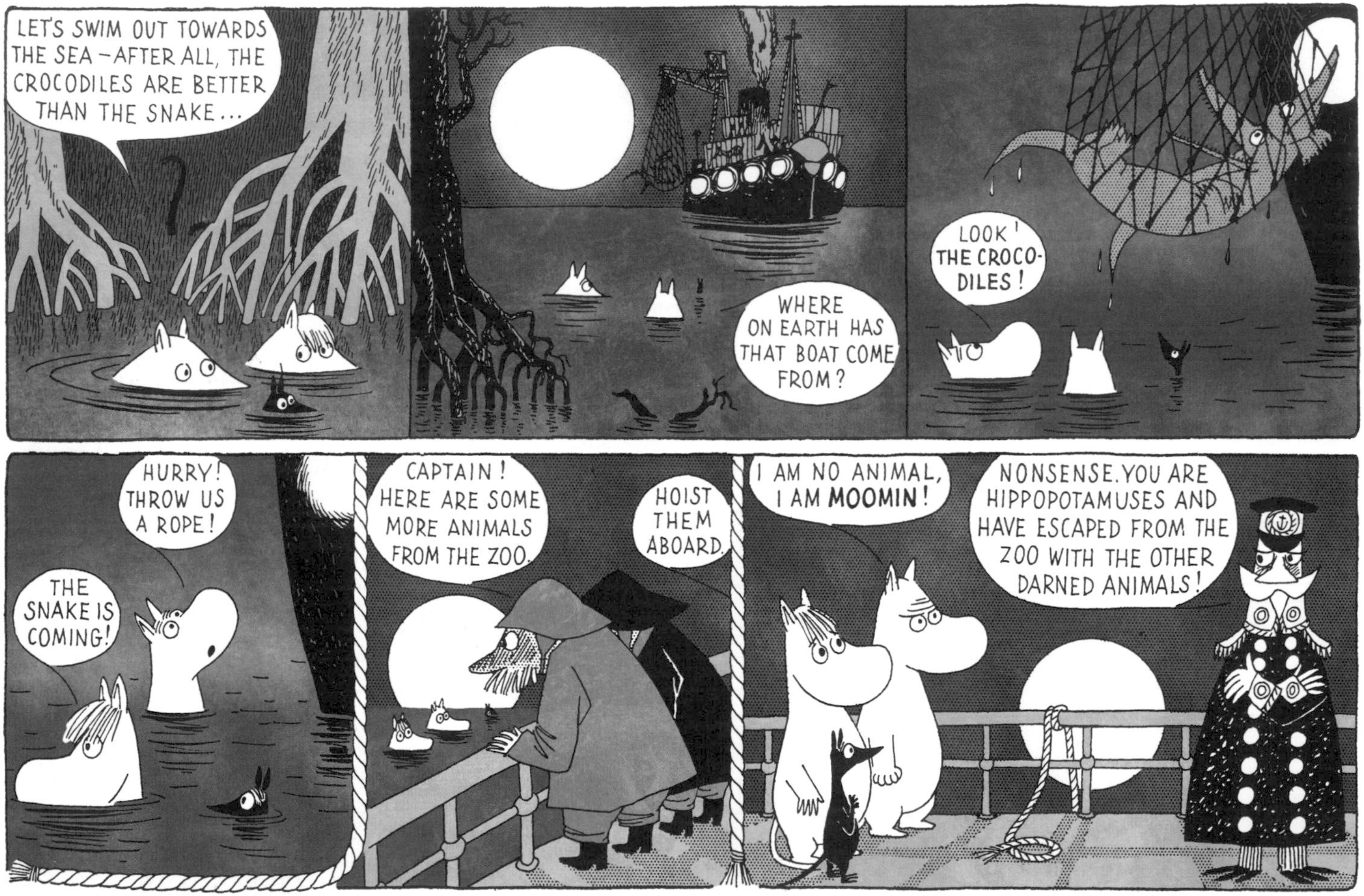
LET'S SWIM OUT TOWARDS THE SEA – AFTER ALL, THE CROCODILES ARE BETTER THAN THE SNAKE ...
WHERE ON EARTH HAS THAT BOAT COME FROM?
LOOK! THE CROCO-DILES!
HURRY! THROW US A ROPE!
THE SNAKE IS COMING!
CAPTAIN! HERE ARE SOME MORE ANIMALS FROM THE ZOO.
HOIST THEM ABOARD.
I AM NO ANIMAL, I AM **MOOMIN**!
NONSENSE. YOU ARE HIPPOPOTAMUSES AND HAVE ESCAPED FROM THE ZOO WITH THE OTHER DARNED ANIMALS!

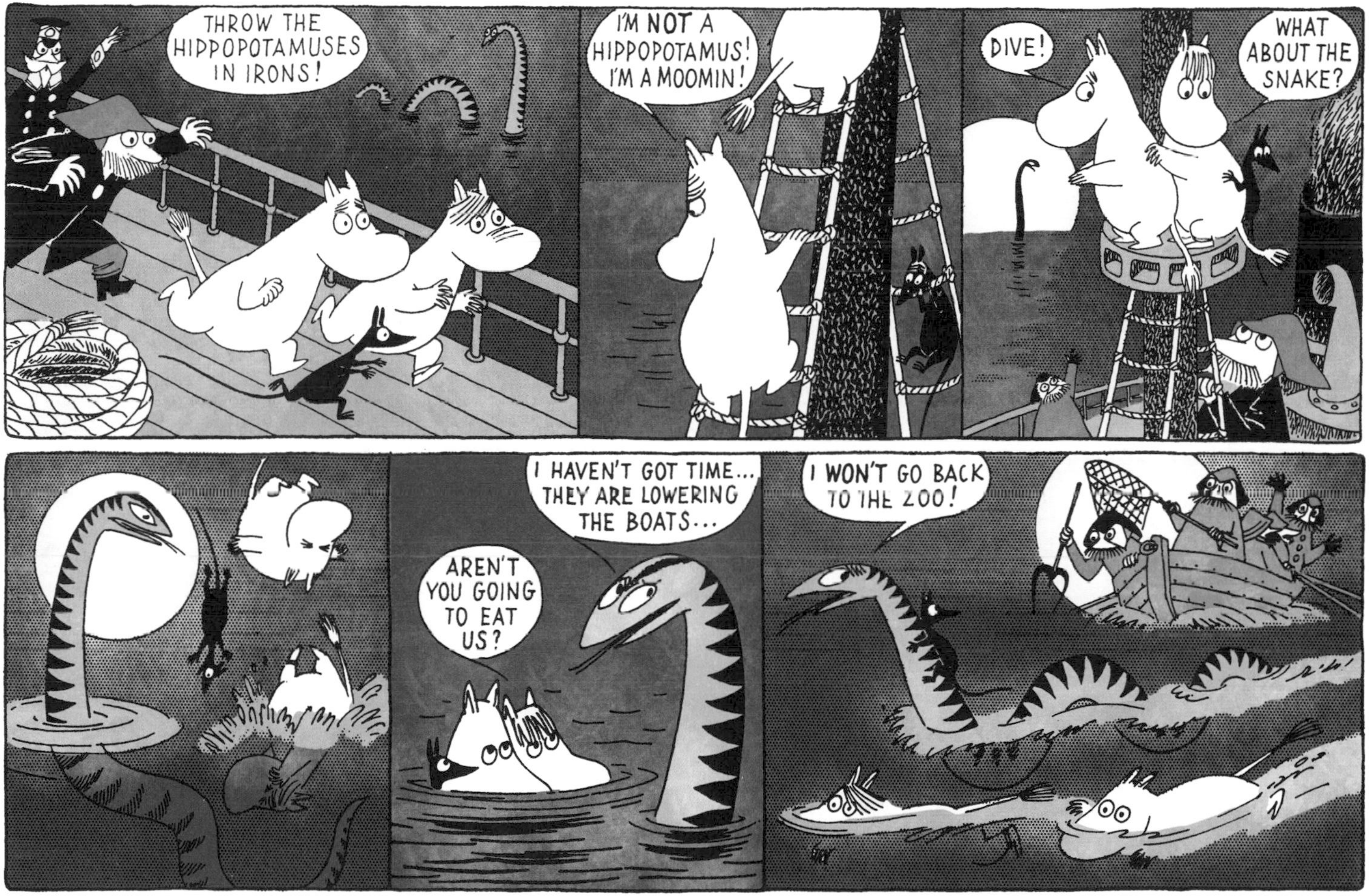
THROW THE HIPPOPOTAMUSES IN IRONS!
I'M NOT A HIPPOPOTAMUS! I'M A MOOMIN!
DIVE!
WHAT ABOUT THE SNAKE?
AREN'T YOU GOING TO EAT US?
I HAVEN'T GOT TIME... THEY ARE LOWERING THE BOATS...
I WON'T GO BACK TO THE ZOO!

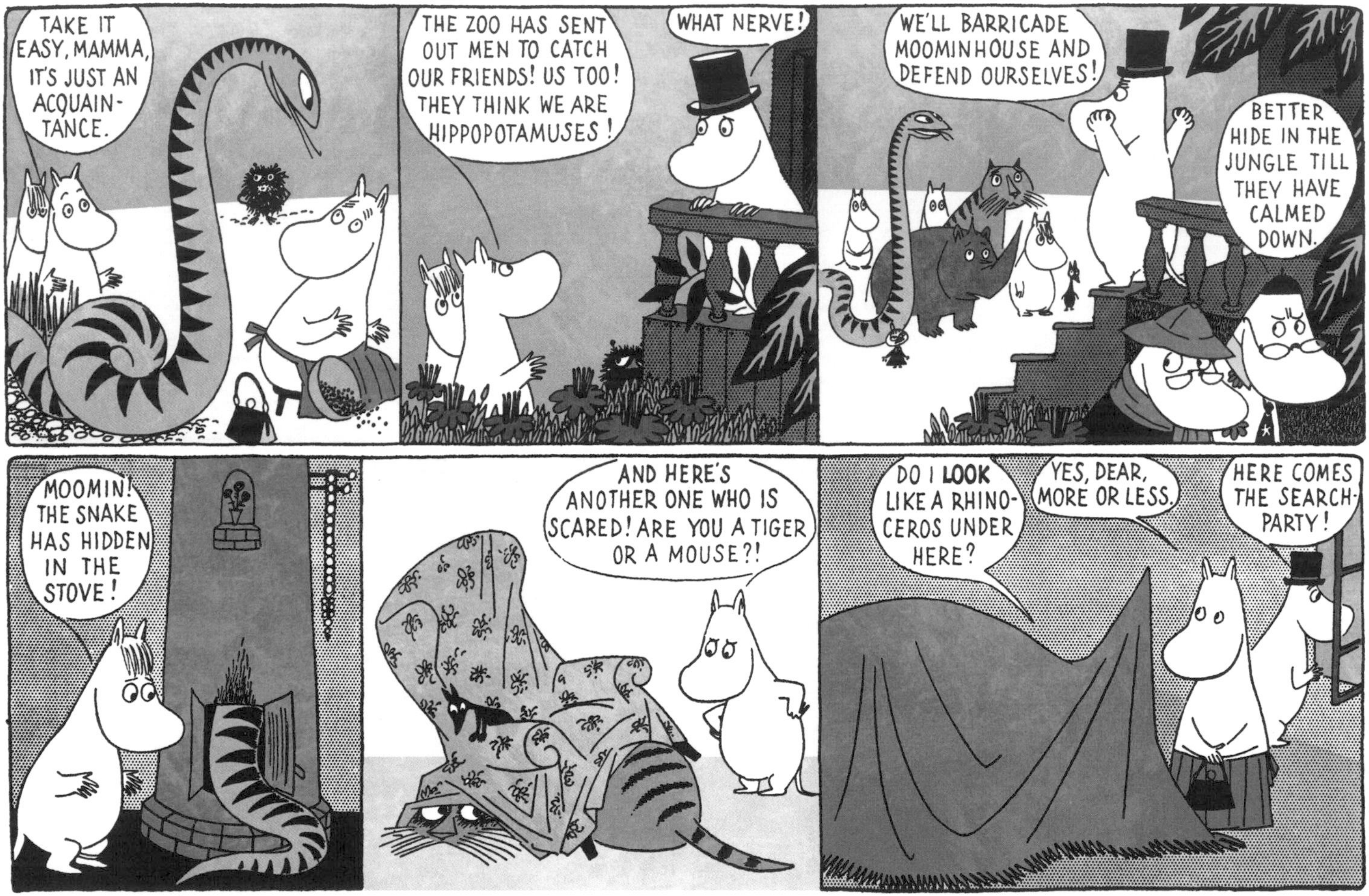
TAKE IT EASY, MAMMA, IT'S JUST AN ACQUAIN-TANCE.
THE ZOO HAS SENT OUT MEN TO CATCH OUR FRIENDS! US TOO! THEY THINK WE ARE HIPPOPOTAMUSES!
WHAT NERVE!
WE'LL BARRICADE MOOMINHOUSE AND DEFEND OURSELVES!
BETTER HIDE IN THE JUNGLE TILL THEY HAVE CALMED DOWN.
MOOMIN! THE SNAKE HAS HIDDEN IN THE STOVE!
AND HERE'S ANOTHER ONE WHO IS SCARED! ARE YOU A TIGER OR A MOUSE?!
DO I **LOOK** LIKE A RHINO-CEROS UNDER HERE?
YES, DEAR, MORE OR LESS.
HERE COMES THE SEARCH-PARTY!

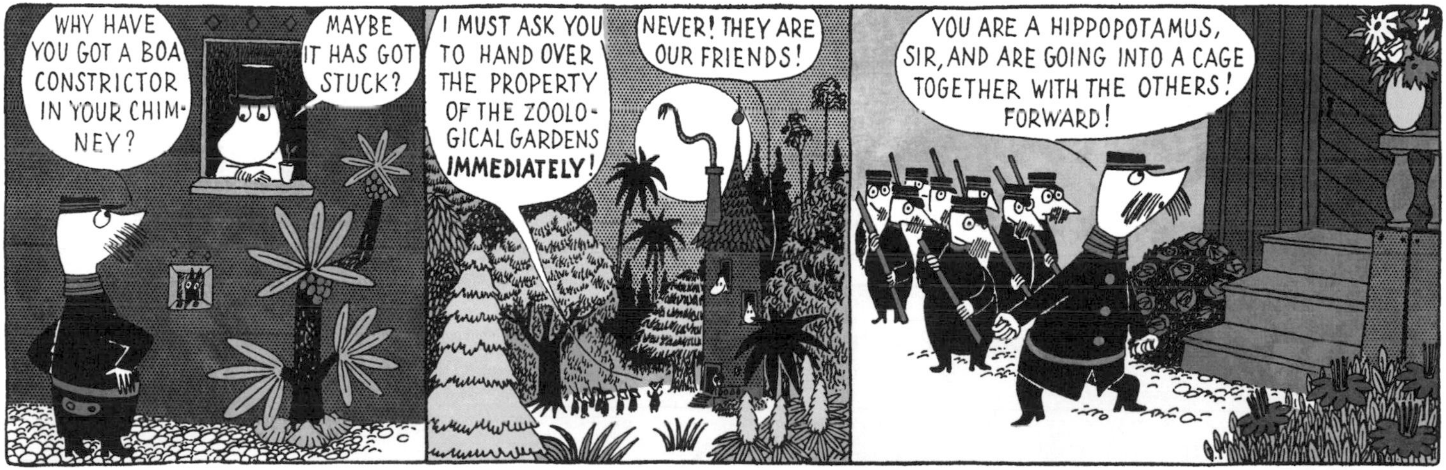
WHY HAVE YOU GOT A BOA CONSTRICTOR IN YOUR CHIM-NEY?
MAYBE IT HAS GOT STUCK?
I MUST ASK YOU TO HAND OVER THE PROPERTY OF THE ZOOLO-GICAL GARDENS **IMMEDIATELY**!
NEVER! THEY ARE OUR FRIENDS!
YOU ARE A HIPPOPOTAMUS, SIR, AND ARE GOING INTO A CAGE TOGETHER WITH THE OTHERS! FORWARD!

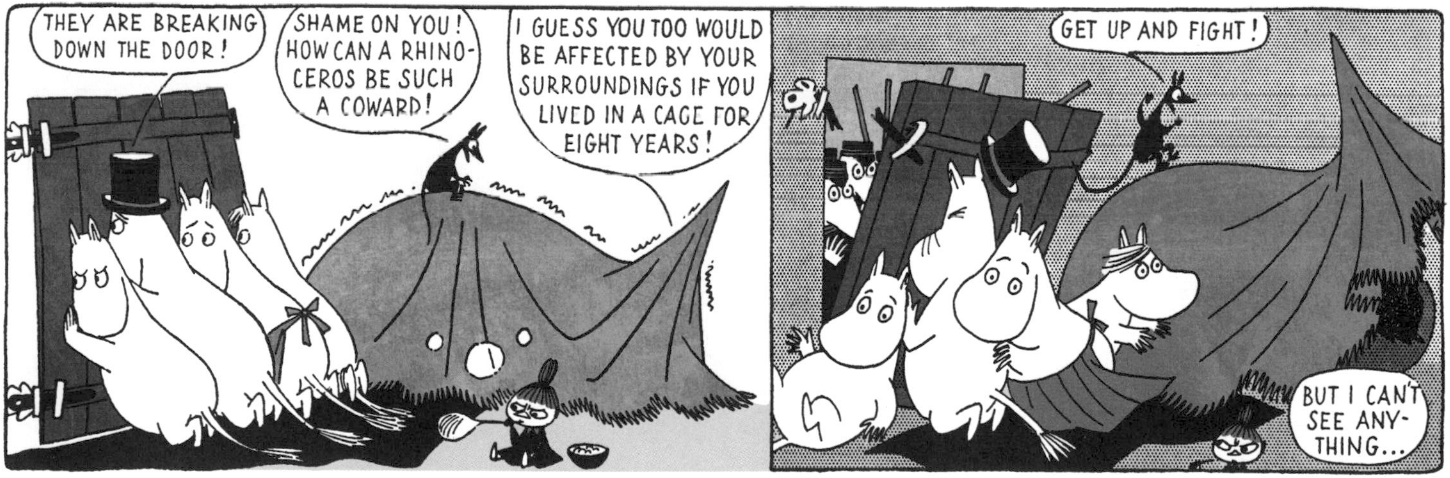
THEY ARE BREAKING DOWN THE DOOR!
SHAME ON YOU! HOW CAN A RHINO-CEROS BE SUCH A COWARD!
I GUESS YOU TOO WOULD BE AFFECTED BY YOUR SURROUNDINGS IF YOU LIVED IN A CAGE FOR EIGHT YEARS!
GET UP AND FIGHT!
BUT I CAN'T SEE ANY-THING...

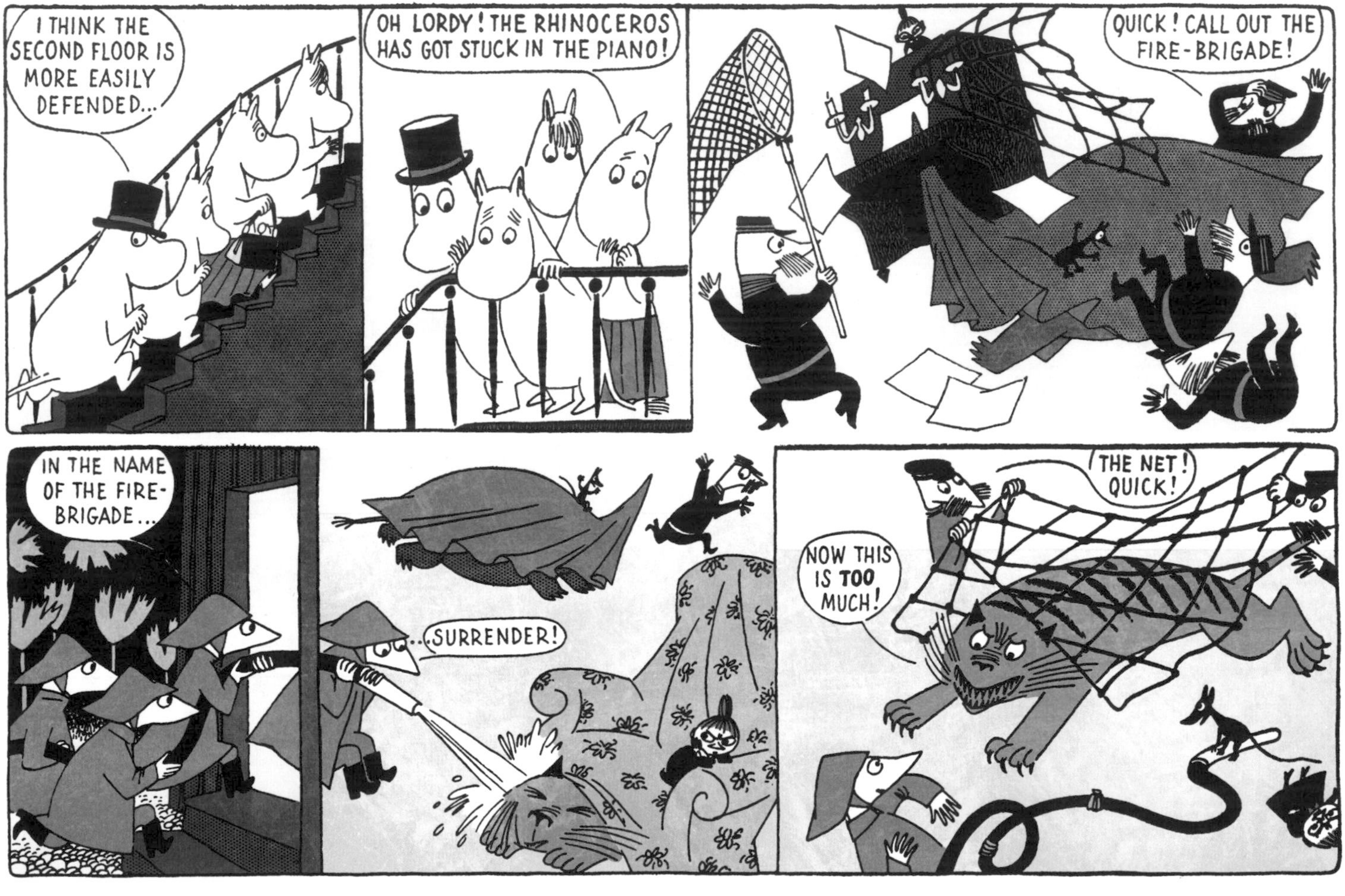
I THINK THE SECOND FLOOR IS MORE EASILY DEFENDED...
OH LORDY! THE RHINOCEROS HAS GOT STUCK IN THE PIANO!
QUICK! CALL OUT THE FIRE-BRIGADE!
IN THE NAME OF THE FIRE-BRIGADE...
...SURRENDER!
THE NET! QUICK!
NOW THIS IS **TOO** MUCH!

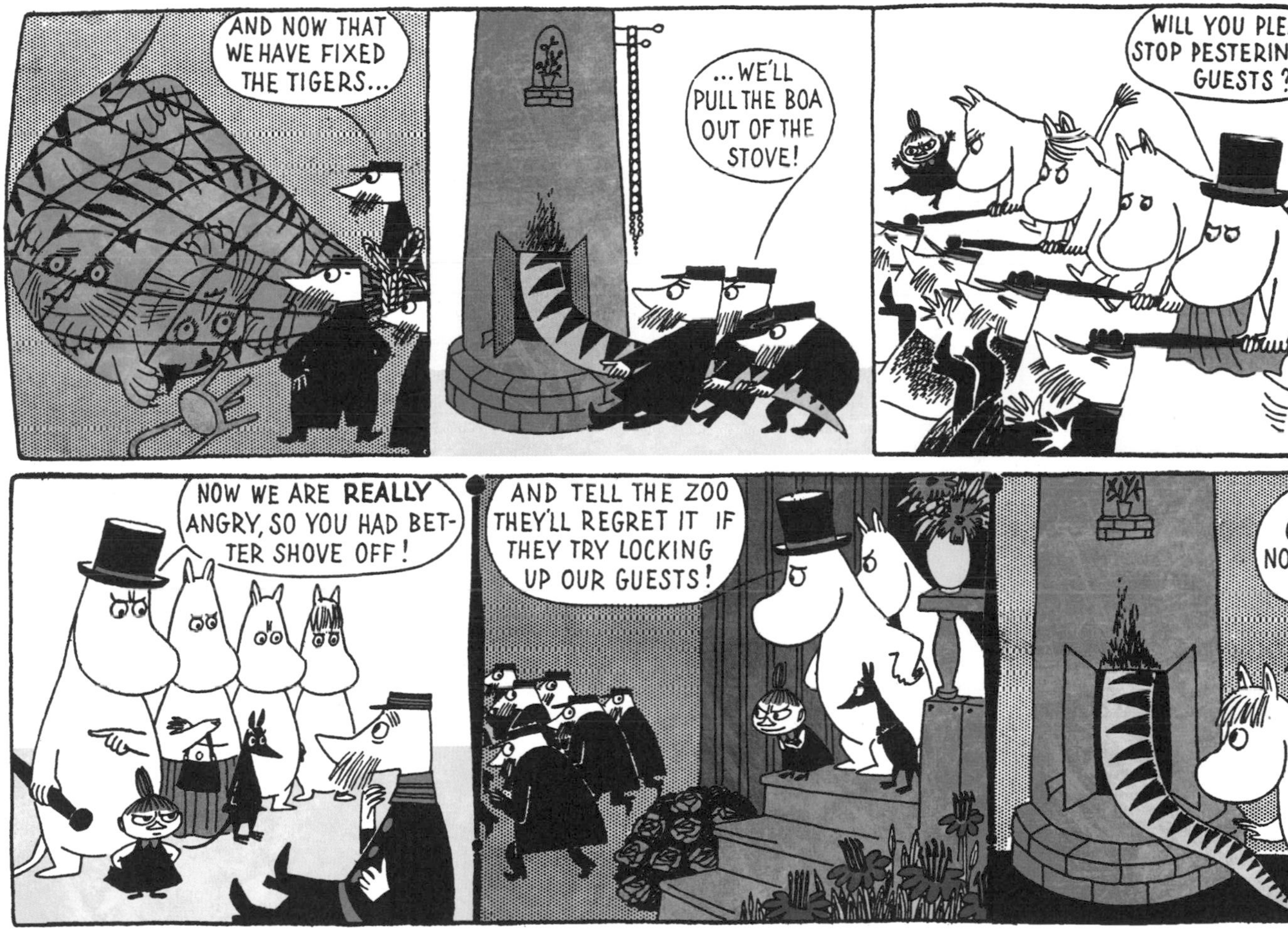
AND NOW THAT WE HAVE FIXED THE TIGERS...
...WE'LL PULL THE BOA OUT OF THE STOVE!
WILL YOU PLEASE STOP PESTERING OUR GUESTS?
NOW WE ARE **REALLY** ANGRY, SO YOU HAD BET-TER SHOVE OFF!
AND TELL THE ZOO THEY'LL REGRET IT IF THEY TRY LOCKING UP OUR GUESTS!
YOU CAN COME OUT NOW! THEY'RE GONE.

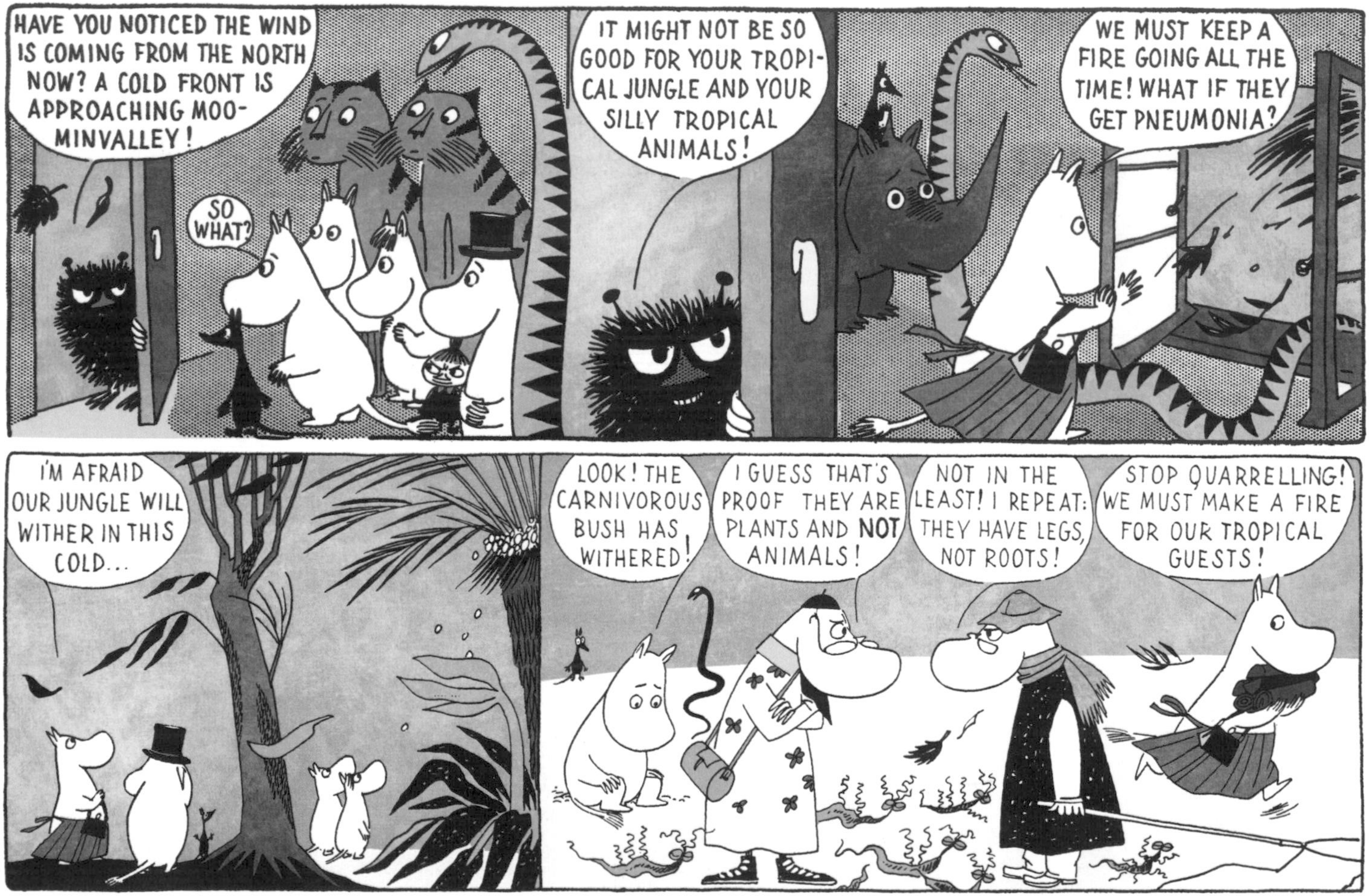
HAVE YOU NOTICED THE WIND IS COMING FROM THE NORTH NOW? A COLD FRONT IS APPROACHING MOOMINVALLEY!
SO WHAT?
IT MIGHT NOT BE SO GOOD FOR YOUR TROPICAL JUNGLE AND YOUR SILLY TROPICAL ANIMALS!
WE MUST KEEP A FIRE GOING ALL THE TIME! WHAT IF THEY GET PNEUMONIA?
I'M AFRAID OUR JUNGLE WILL WITHER IN THIS COLD...
LOOK! THE CARNIVOROUS BUSH HAS WITHERED!
I GUESS THAT'S PROOF THEY ARE PLANTS AND NOT ANIMALS!
NOT IN THE LEAST! I REPEAT: THEY HAVE LEGS, NOT ROOTS!
STOP QUARRELLING! WE MUST MAKE A FIRE FOR OUR TROPICAL GUESTS!

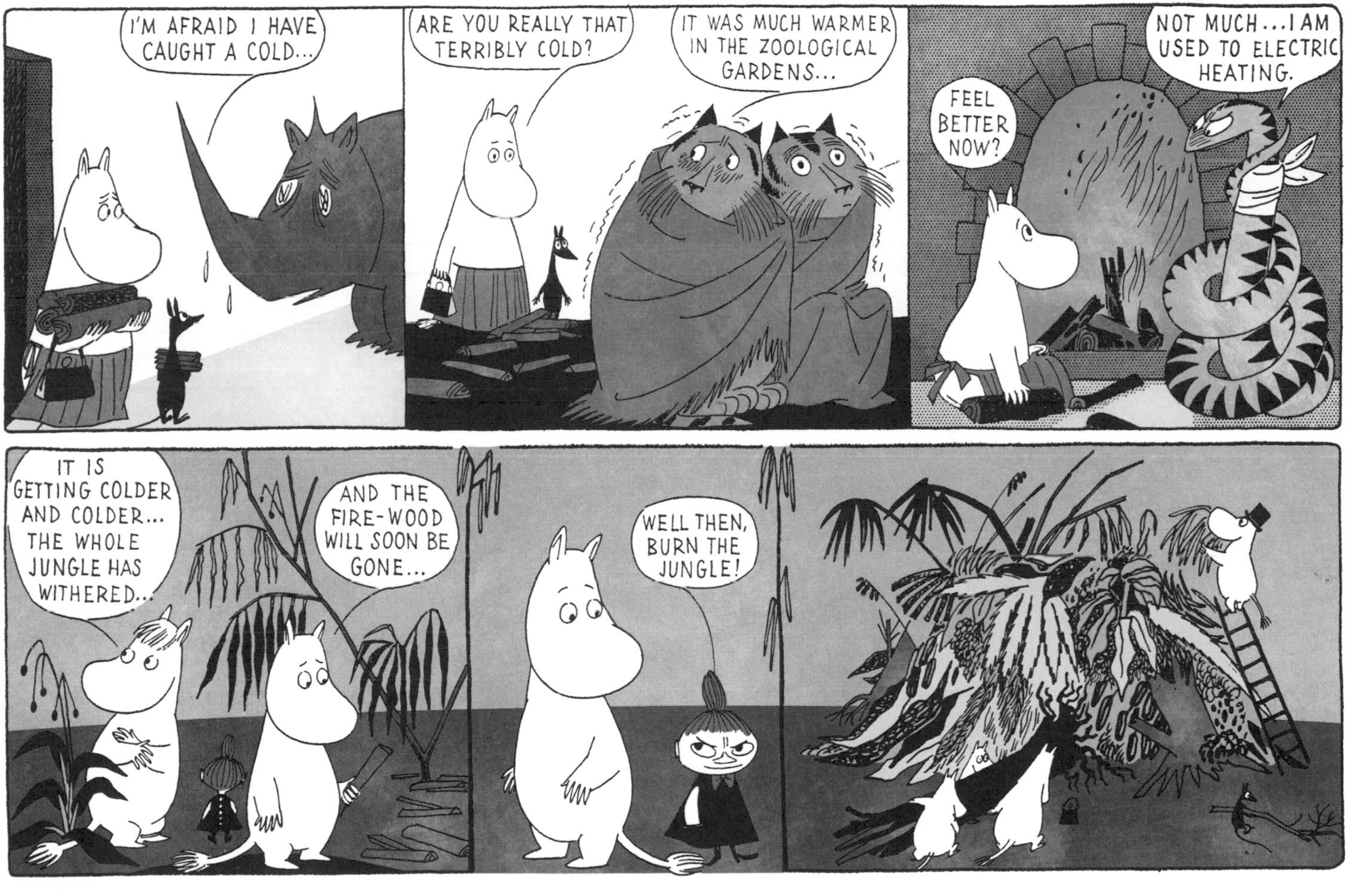
I'M AFRAID I HAVE CAUGHT A COLD...
ARE YOU REALLY THAT TERRIBLY COLD?
IT WAS MUCH WARMER IN THE ZOOLOGICAL GARDENS...
FEEL BETTER NOW?
NOT MUCH...I AM USED TO ELECTRIC HEATING.
IT IS GETTING COLDER AND COLDER... THE WHOLE JUNGLE HAS WITHERED...
AND THE FIRE-WOOD WILL SOON BE GONE...
WELL THEN, BURN THE JUNGLE!

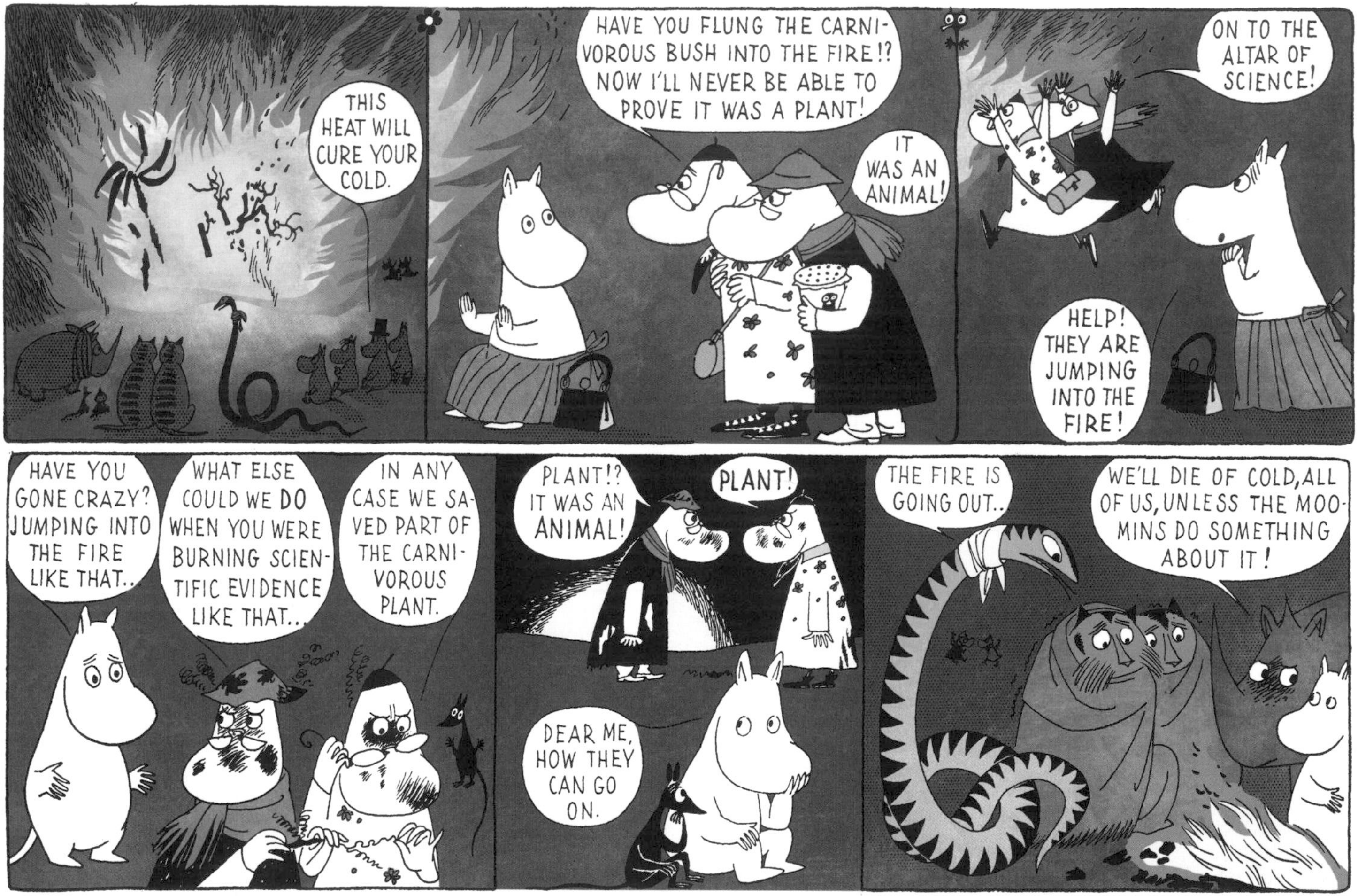
THIS HEAT WILL CURE YOUR COLD.
HAVE YOU FLUNG THE CARNI-VOROUS BUSH INTO THE FIRE!? NOW I'LL NEVER BE ABLE TO PROVE IT WAS A PLANT!
IT WAS AN ANIMAL!
ON TO THE ALTAR OF SCIENCE!
HELP! THEY ARE JUMPING INTO THE FIRE!
HAVE YOU GONE CRAZY? JUMPING INTO THE FIRE LIKE THAT..
WHAT ELSE COULD WE DO WHEN YOU WERE BURNING SCIEN-TIFIC EVIDENCE LIKE THAT..
IN ANY CASE WE SA-VED PART OF THE CARNI-VOROUS PLANT.
PLANT!? IT WAS AN ANIMAL!
PLANT!
DEAR ME, HOW THEY CAN GO ON.
THE FIRE IS GOING OUT..
WE'LL DIE OF COLD, ALL OF US, UNLESS THE MOO-MINS DO SOMETHING ABOUT IT!

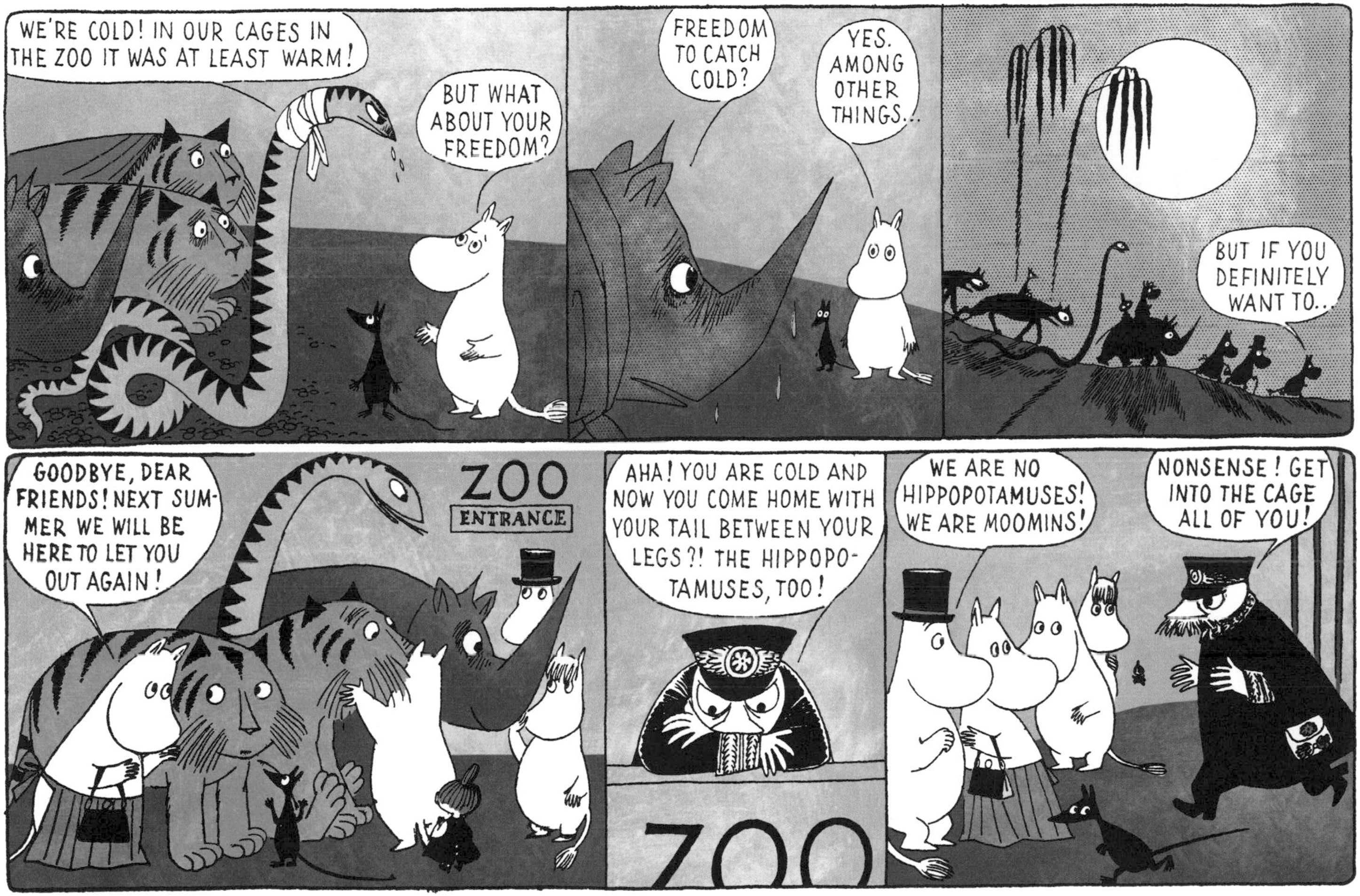
WE'RE COLD! IN OUR CAGES IN THE ZOO IT WAS AT LEAST WARM!
BUT WHAT ABOUT YOUR FREEDOM?
FREEDOM TO CATCH COLD?
YES. AMONG OTHER THINGS...
BUT IF YOU DEFINITELY WANT TO...
GOODBYE, DEAR FRIENDS! NEXT SUMMER WE WILL BE HERE TO LET YOU OUT AGAIN!
ZOO
ENTRANCE
AHA! YOU ARE COLD AND NOW YOU COME HOME WITH YOUR TAIL BETWEEN YOUR LEGS?! THE HIPPOPOTAMUSES, TOO!
ZOO
WE ARE NO HIPPOPOTAMUSES! WE ARE MOOMINS!
NONSENSE! GET INTO THE CAGE ALL OF YOU!

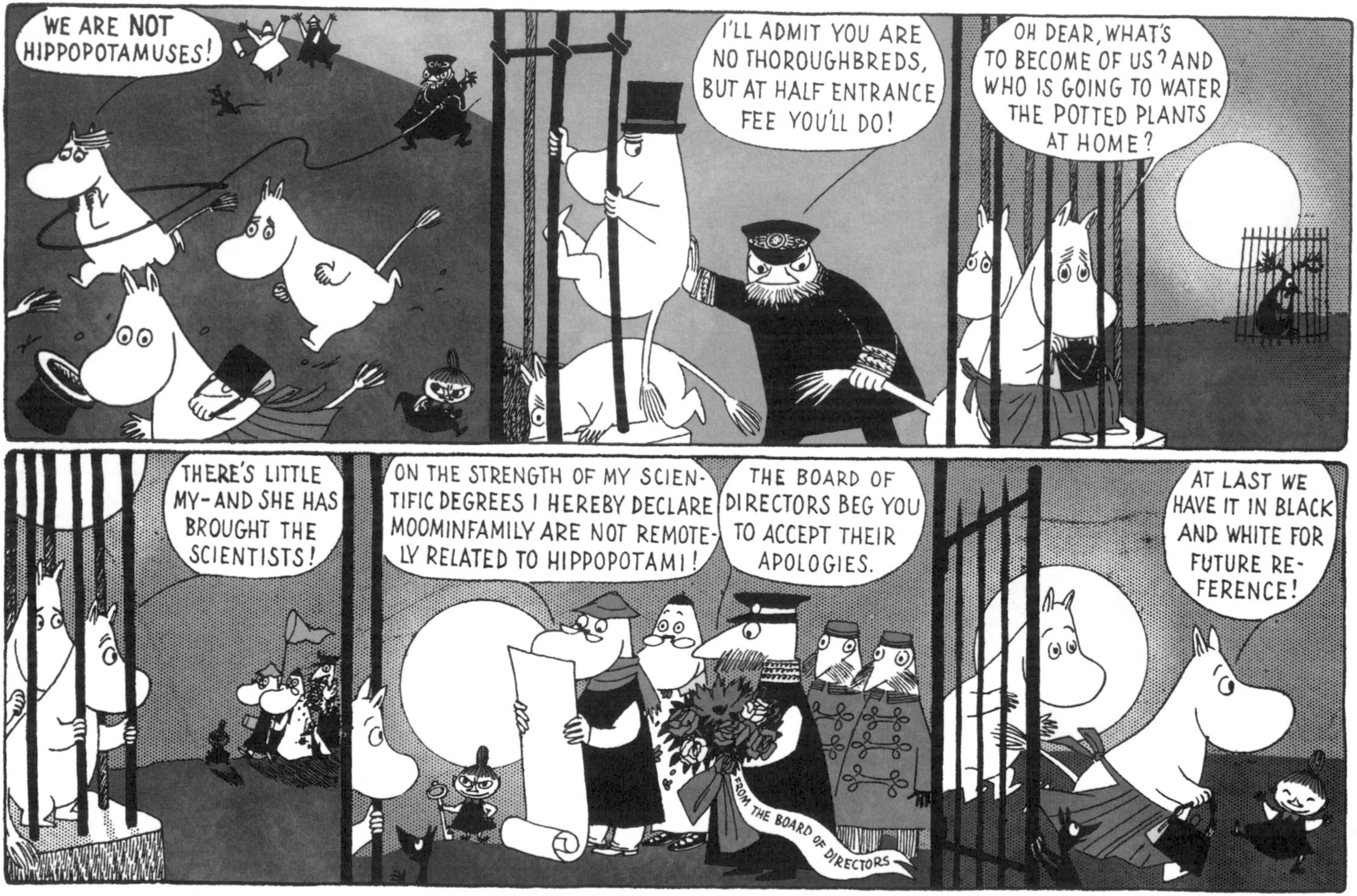

WE ARE NOT HIPPOPOTAMUSES!
I'LL ADMIT YOU ARE NO THOROUGHBREDS, BUT AT HALF ENTRANCE FEE YOU'LL DO!
OH DEAR, WHAT'S TO BECOME OF US? AND WHO IS GOING TO WATER THE POTTED PLANTS AT HOME?
THERE'S LITTLE MY- AND SHE HAS BROUGHT THE SCIENTISTS!
ON THE STRENGTH OF MY SCIENTIFIC DEGREES I HEREBY DECLARE MOOMINFAMILY ARE NOT REMOTELY RELATED TO HIPPOPOTAMI!
THE BOARD OF DIRECTORS BEG YOU TO ACCEPT THEIR APOLOGIES.
FROM THE BOARD OF DIRECTORS
AT LAST WE HAVE IT IN BLACK AND WHITE FOR FUTURE REFERENCE!

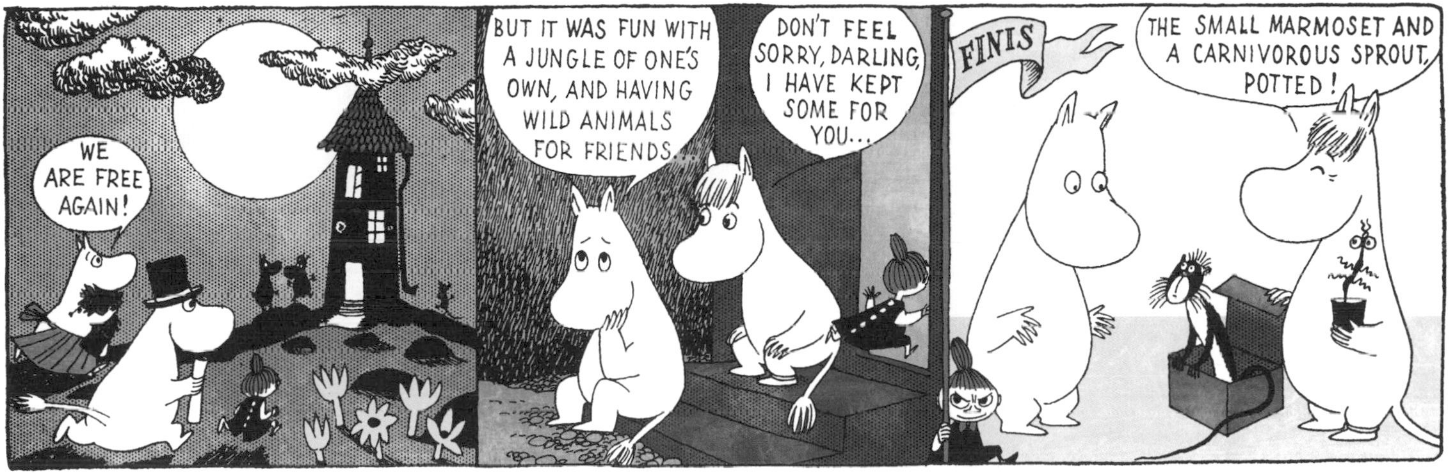
WE ARE FREE AGAIN!
BUT IT WAS FUN WITH A JUNGLE OF ONE'S OWN, AND HAVING WILD ANIMALS FOR FRIENDS...
DON'T FEEL SORRY, DARLING, I HAVE KEPT SOME FOR YOU...
FINIS
THE SMALL MARMOSET AND A CARNIVOROUS SPROUT, POTTED!

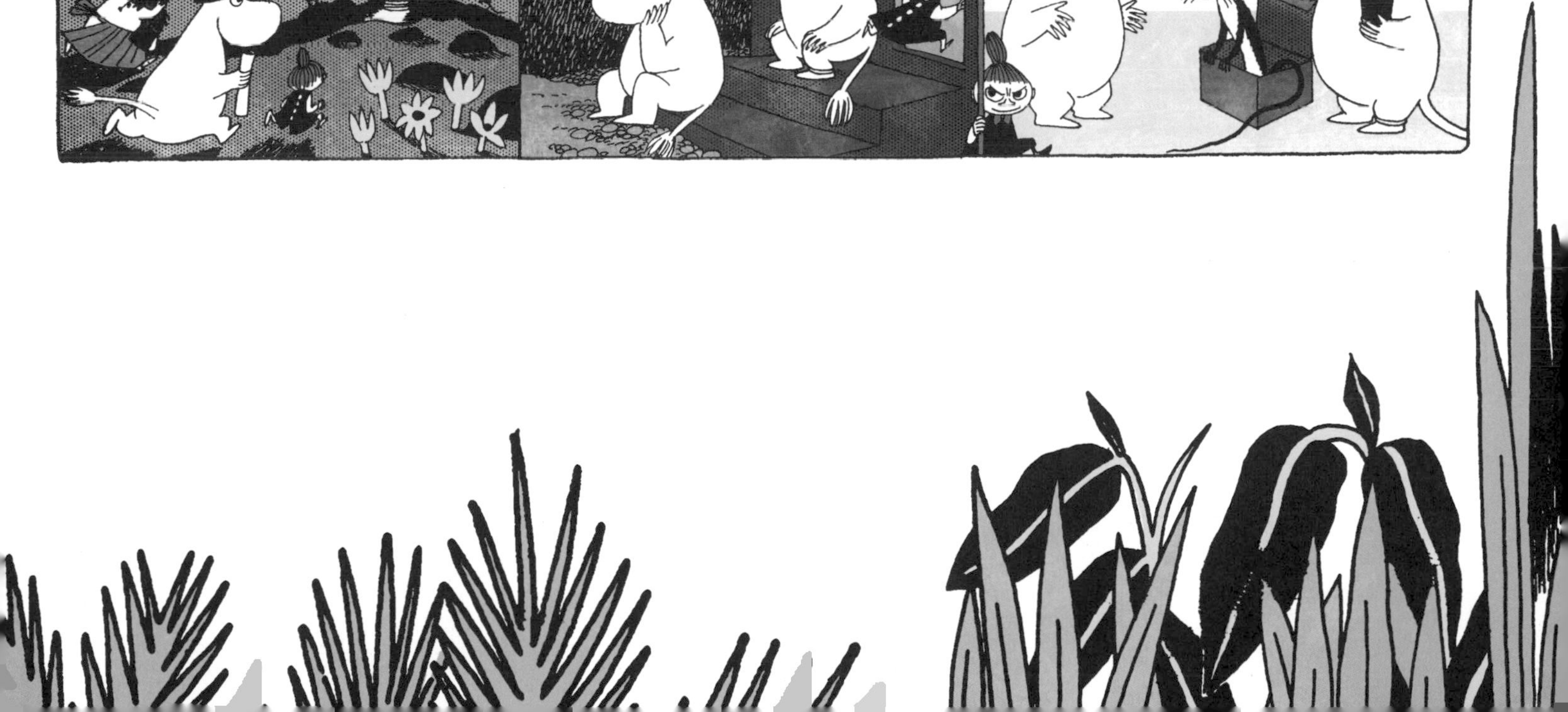

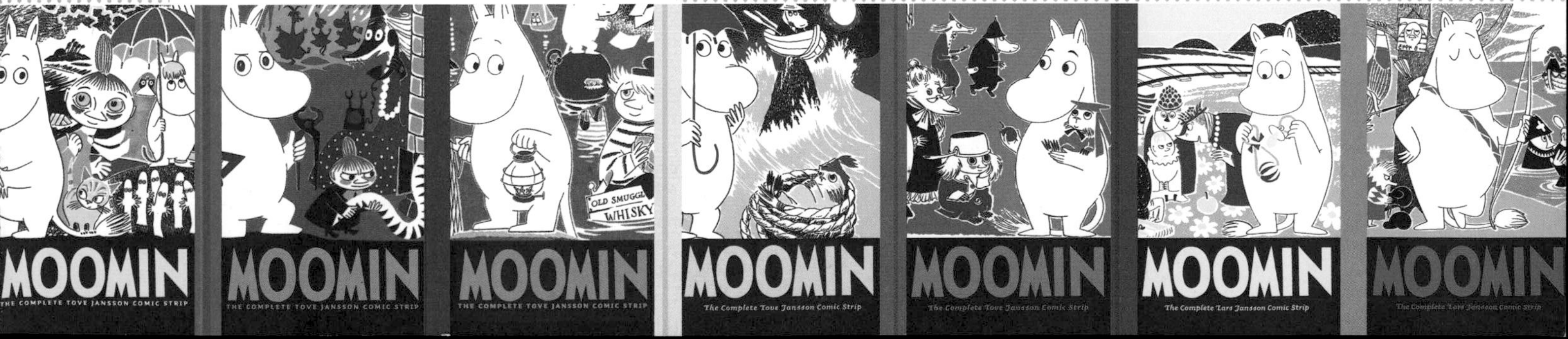
MOOMIN
THE COMPLETE TOVE JANSSON COMIC STRIP
MOOMIN
THE COMPLETE TOVE JANSSON COMIC STRIP
MOOMIN
THE COMPLETE TOVE JANSSON COMIC STRIP
WHISKY
MOOMIN
The Complete Tove Jansson Comic Strip
MOOMIN
The Complete Tove Jansson Comic Strip
MOOMIN
The Complete Lars Jansson Comic Strip
MOOMIN

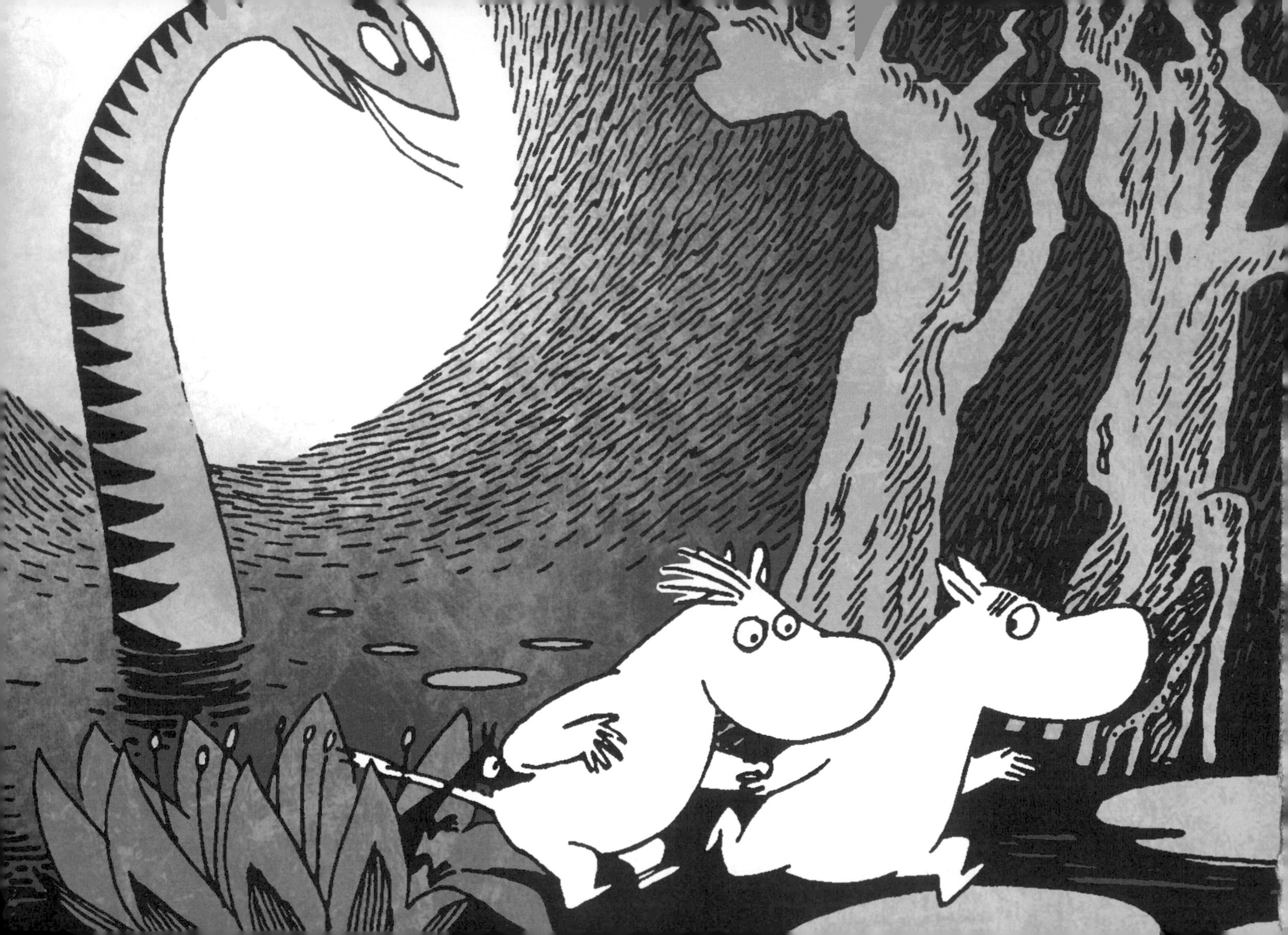

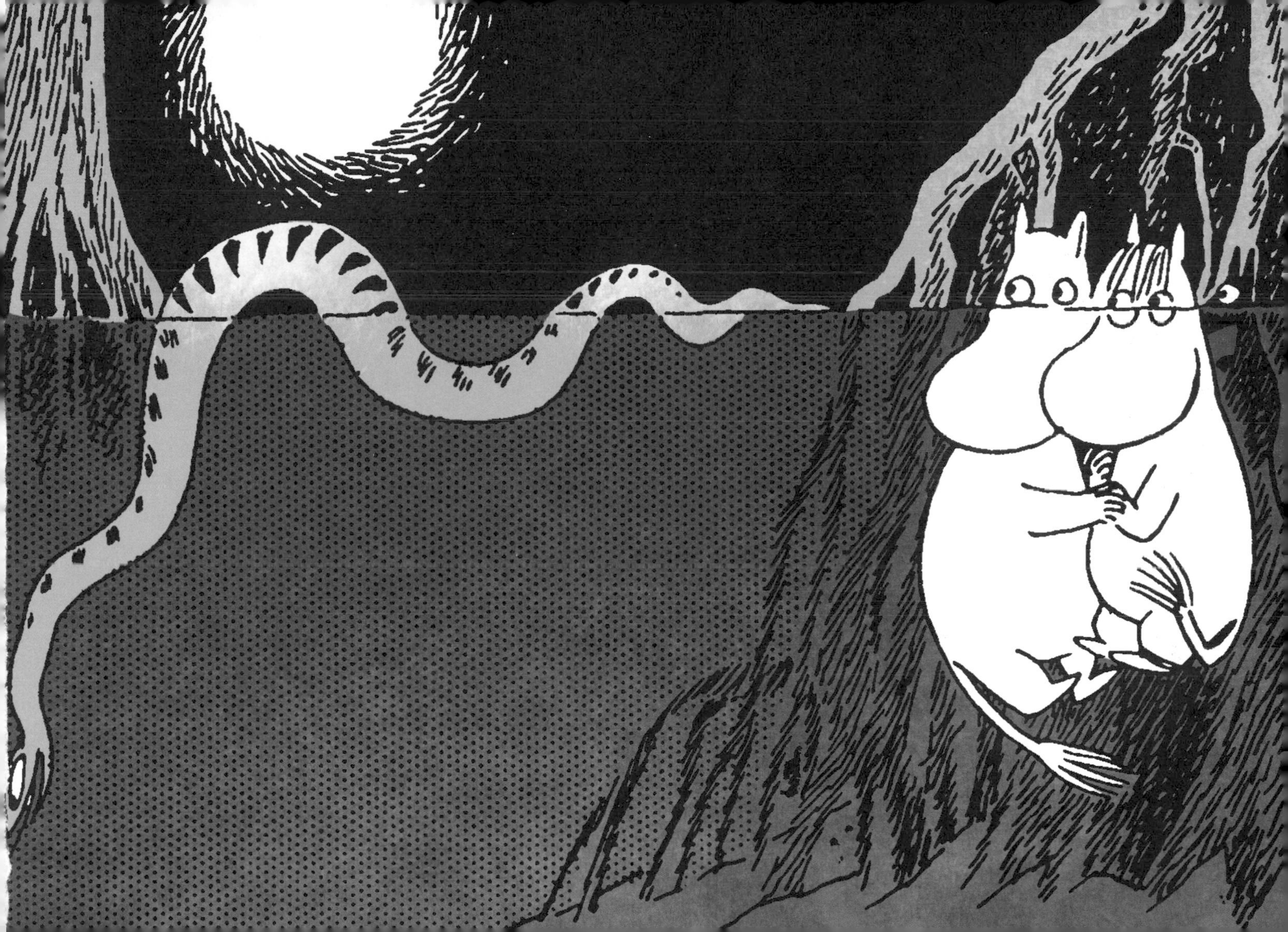

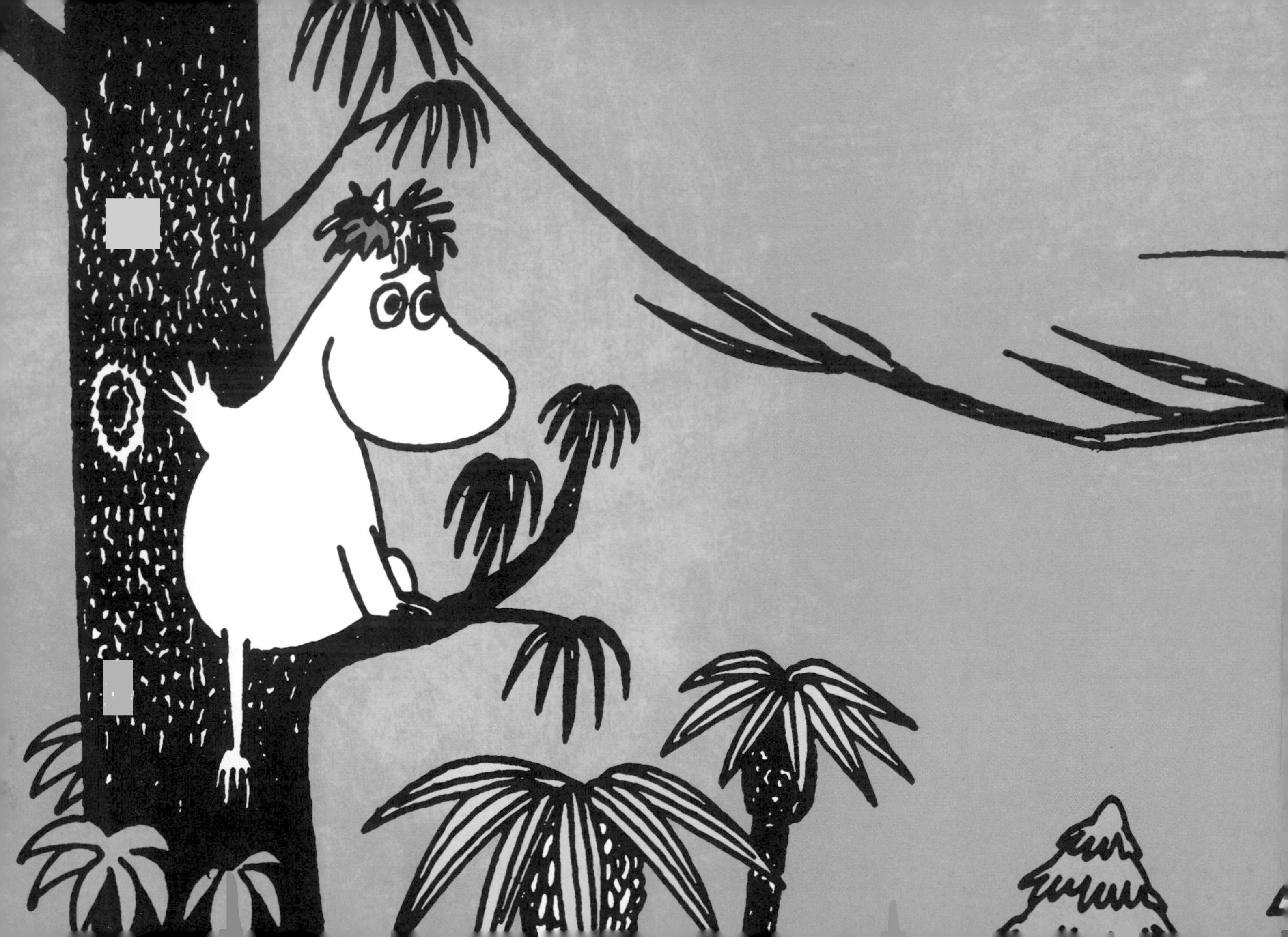